Lewis Woolston grew up in Geraldton, Western Australia. Hating it, he left as soon as he could. He misspent most of his youth in Perth and Adelaide, undertook a short and miserable stint in the Australian Army, and spent years living and working in remote roadhouses on the Nullarbor and in the Northern Territory before settling down. Truth Serum Press published Lewis's first collection *The Last Free Man and Other Stories* (2019), which was shortlisted for Best Fiction in the 2020 Chief Minister's NT Book Awards, and followed this with *Remembering the Dead and Other Stories* (2022). He lives in Port Lincoln, South Australia, with his wife and daughter.

THE EVERLASTING

AND OTHER STORIES

LEWIS WOOLSTON

TRUTH SERUM PRESS

ISBN: 978-1-923000-61-2

BP#00135

Truth Serum Press
32 Meredith Street
Sefton Park SA 5083
Australia

Email: truthserumpress@live.com.au
Website: truthserumpress.net
Truth Serum Press catalogue: truthserumpress.net/catalogue

Cover design copyright © Matt Potter
Cover image *Poonindie, 2024* copyright © Lewis Woolston
Author photograph © Linsey Berryman, used with permission

Also available as an ePub eBook
ISBN: 978-1-923000-67-4
Also available as a Kindle eBook
ISBN: 978-1-923000-74-2

Truth Serum Press is a member of the
Bequem Publishing collective
bequempublishing.com

With sentimental affection,
this book is dedicated
to my cousin Nicole.

I hope you find
your little slice of
happily ever after.

CONTENTS

YOU'LL ALWAYS REMEMBER FREMANTLE

He dreamt of home again. At night, in his uncomfortable metal bunk onboard the HMAS Parramatta out at sea, his unconscious mind took him back home.

It was becoming more regular this nightly journey back to home and family. He began to suspect, quietly to himself only, that he was deeply homesick and ought never to have joined the Navy. He'd been in less than a year and he wondered that if he was already feeling this way now what would he be like towards the end of the four-year stint he'd signed up for?

The dreams were more or less the same every time. He was back home with his parents in the little fibro house they lived in. Or more often they were in the Gawler Baptist Church where his father was the minister. The old stone building as familiar to him as his own face. The place where he'd spent so much of his youth, carefully guided by the loving hands of his father and mother.

His father was giving a sermon in this dream. Up there in the old pulpit giving THE WORD in his deep and loud but thoroughly gentle voice. A voice one parishioner had once described as a "nicer version of Johnny Cash sort of voice," a description that made total sense to everyone in the congregation.

In this dream his father was preaching from 2 Corinthians 4:7-18, an old favourite of his, a particular hobby horse you might say. The temporary nature of this life, the eternal glory to come, the trial of this world that must be endured faithfully first. It was his favourite theme and his congregation had heard it from him before.

He'd heard it at home from his father and mother too, the better version, the full story behind the scripture. How his father had been born into an old money family in Adelaide. People who owned property, people who knew State Premiers and business people, people who lived a life of comfort and pleasure. How his father had "felt the call" as a teenager and wondered if there wasn't something more to life than the acquisition of money and property. How he'd broken with a century and a half of family history and studied at Bible College instead of Law or Accounting. How he'd moved to Sri Lanka with a Baptist Mission group and worked tirelessly for the people there and the salvation of their souls. His family had washed their hands of him, disinherited him. He always told the story so dramatically, "Washed their hands of me, barred their door to me, forever!" he'd boom in his Prophet's voice.

Young Jones was always impressed at that part of the story. His father had chosen exile, poverty and the status of an orphan over the pleasures of the world and he'd done so for Christ. An epic sacrifice that he would always live in the shadow of.

For his father and mother had met in Sri Lanka, both working for the Baptist Mission, they'd fallen in love but not acted on it for nearly a decade believing the work they were doing was more important than their own personal happiness. Their marriage was delayed until they had given the better part of their youth to the Mission. Then they'd moved back to Australia. Young Jones was the only child of their union, the lateness of their marriage meant there could be no more children for them. They'd given their youth and their fertility to the Mission but did not complain. They believed the sacrifice was more than worth it "for this momentary light affliction is producing for us an eternal weight of glory beyond all comparison" as his father was fond of quoting.

The ship's PA broke his dreaming. He quickly dressed like he'd been taught at basic training. Smithy walked down the hallway and told him what was happening. Smithy always knew what was happening.

'Old Man wants us manning the rails when we come in to Fremantle. Respect for the Port City or some shit like that. Just make sure your uniform is correct and you'll be right, mate.'

He adjusted Jones's collar and seemed satisfied.

'Word is we're all getting a little day leave in Fremantle, Young Jonesy; fucken Freo, you little beauty! Best port in Australia, if you ask me. Sydney is nice but it's stupidly expensive, Darwin is a shithole, Melbourne is cold and grim and Hobart is completely pointless. Fremantle has it all and has it better in my experience. Stick with me, Young Jonesy, and we'll get that cherry of yours popped for sure!'

Jones groaned inwardly. A week or so ago he'd had a beer too many in the mess and confessed to Smithy that he was a virgin. After much laughter and ribbing Smithy had promised him he would get his condition fixed at the next port. Jones was quietly dreading what might happen once they got ashore.

They got themselves in order and joined the others manning the rails as the ship sailed into Fremantle Harbour.

Young Jones thought of his parents again. How they'd reacted when he told them that he wanted to join the Navy.

His father wanted to know why? What was appealing about the Navy? Young Jones had struggled to explain himself.

3

'It's just, I kind of want to do something meaningful, noble … sort of … heroic.'

The words had struggled to come out and sounded silly in his own ears when he'd said them. His father, to his credit, didn't dismiss this urge of his son's, thought it a good impulse in fact; he just questioned if the Navy was the right vehicle for the ambition his son expressed.

'The days of saving the world from Nazis or Japs are long gone, son. You'll mostly be doing pointless patrols looking for refugees up north or off the coast of Somalia trying to stop pirates. A lot of the time you'll just be training for things that never happen and having to endure hardships for no real purpose. A lot of what the Military does in peace time is tedious and less than glamourous.'

Young Jones had nodded agreement to his father but in his heart he was not convinced.

'I understand that you want to do something worthwhile and noble with your life, son. That desire does you credit and I'm proud of you but is the Military really the best place to achieve that goal? What about the Ministry? Your Mother and I gave twenty years of our lives to a Mission in Sri Lanka and it fulfilled us. I mean that, son. We helped deliver babies, looked after children, held the hands of the dying as they passed into the next world. We built things, we made a difference, a real difference. Even now as the Minister of this old church here in Gawler, I make a difference. The Ministry is fulfilling, it gives your life purpose, if that's what you're looking for.'

Young Jones had tried to speak then, opened his mouth to say things he had felt for a very long time. He meekly shook his head instead.

'I just want to see a bit of the world.'

It was the best he could do at the time. His father had the good sense to realise that further disagreement was futile and would probably backfire. He'd agreed to sign the forms giving parental consent and at the tender age of 17, Young Jones joined the Navy.

Now here he was manning the rails of the HMAS Parramatta as they entered Fremantle Harbour with the promise of shore leave and the terror of losing his virginity.

They'd been granted their shore leave just as Smithy predicted. Smithy was always spot on about everything that happened on the ship. Smithy was a Navy lifer who despite being in for ten years hadn't managed to rise in rank beyond an ordinary sailor. Smithy had taken Young Jones under his wing and tried to set him straight about how the Navy worked.

To Smithy the Navy was merely an elaborate way for a working bloke like him to milk the Australian taxpayer for a living and a comfortable retirement. It was one of his often-repeated phrases whenever he seemed to be living well or scoring one off the system "Gawd bless the Australian Taxpayer," he'd say as if they'd personally handed him a big cheque or a cold beer.

The officers loathed Smithy most of the time, called him a "barracks room lawyer" due to his habit of knowing rules and regulations better than they themselves did. They were forever trying to catch him out so they could punish him and possibly get him kicked out of the Navy entirely but Smithy, in his ten years of service, had learnt every trick there possibly could be. He managed to maintain a basically clean disciplinary record while scamming the Navy for everything he could while slacking off as much as he could. No small achievement.

The officer on the gangway grimaced when he saw Smithy approaching. They showed him their leave passes and he grunted his assent.

'Don't let this shitbag corrupt you, Young Jonesy; you're a good lad and he'll only lead you astray.'

'It's all good, sir,' Smithy claimed. 'I've taken him under my wing and I'll keep him out of trouble.' Every syllable was a subtle "fuck you" to the officer.

The Officer glared at him.

'He's just salty the Old Man has got him on public relations duties,' said Smithy once they were on dry land. 'They're opening the ship to the public, letting all the stupid kids have a look in the hope that they'll want to join up. Guess who got stuck with supervising that bullshit? Stupid cunt.'

The long line of sailors in uniform straggled towards the gate and into Fremantle. They talked loudly, full of life and boisterous good humour, cheerfully hanging shit on each other with the happy, easy familiarity of men who've been cooped up on a ship for months. A day of shore leave was a treasure for these men.

Young Jones insisted on stopping at the Post Office much to Smithy's disgust.

'I'll just get a postcard off to my parents and then we'll keep going.' Smithy rolled his eyes and said 'go on then' and Young Jones raced inside.

He found a nice postcard with an aerial view of Fremantle on it. He paid for it and a stamp and then retired to the little desk with the pens on chains. He wrote out some quick banalities and carefully added the address. Smithy was still waiting outside when he posted it in the big red mailbox.

'C'mon let's go, we've got a woman waiting to make a man of you, son, and you're dragging your feet like it's kitchen duty.'

Jones tried and failed to look like he was at ease as he walked along with Smithy. Crossing and uncrossing his arms, putting his hands in his pockets, anything to appear less nervous than he actually was. He noticed the people, the civilians on the street, seemed to accord them some respect because of their uniforms. They made room for them to pass by with a certain deference, the girls looked at them admiringly. For a moment, just a moment, it made Young Jones feel like a man. Like he'd achieved something, like he was a somebody. Then the knowledge of what was about to happen made him feel like a little boy again.

The other men had mostly turned off into various pubs and cafes along the Fremantle strip but they kept walking. Now here they were. 'Ada Rose' the sign said.

'This place is a piece of history. Been around forever. You know this place stayed open all through the years when it was illegal? The WA Police Commissioner at the time was a veteran himself and this joint had and still has a policy of ten percent discount for men in uniform so he let them stay open in spite of what the law said. A lot of blokes on their way to Vietnam got their first or last fucks in this place.'

He stood there and smiled triumphantly before slapping Young Jonesy on the back.

'And now it's your turn, young bloke! C'mon, let's go in and get you sorted.'

They walked in, Smithy confident and in front, a man who'd done this many times before, Young Jones behind him, feeling more like a boy than ever.

The Madam greeted them and they sat down in the waiting room with a complimentary can of Coke each. The Madam asked them if they'd like to see the ladies separately or together.

'Young fella is here by way of making his debut, if you know what I mean, so maybe let him get first pick. You got a nice girl that will go gentle on him? Still missing Mummy and Daddy and the girls at school, you know how it is with young ones.'

Smithy's boisterous voice embarrassed Jones more than the actual revelation about his lack of sexual experience. He wanted to tell him to shut up or at least tone it down. Surely you didn't say such things that loudly? Even in a place like this.

The Madam seemed sympathetic to his plight. She directed her attention from Smithy to Jones and her face had a tender, almost motherly expression of genuine care, or at least that's how Jones interpreted it.

'I have a lady who might suit you, her name is Holly, she's a blonde, petite, very gentle and nice, you'd like her.'

The last bit sounded insistent: you'd like her. A promise? Or a selling point? Young Jones wasn't sure, he didn't entirely understand how this all worked so he nodded that he'd like to see this lady Holly.

'If you'll follow me,' she said to Jones before addressing Smithy. 'The other ladies will come out and introduce themselves shortly.'

Smithy was cheerful about it. 'I'll be fine waiting but just get the young fella sorted,' he said, and waved at Jones like a parent seeing off their child to his first day of school.

She led him into a bedroom and sat him down on the bed.

'Holly will see you in a minute,' she said, and he nodded dumbly.

Holly walked in and he stared at her. She was blonde, skinny but in a natural healthy sort of way, at ease with the situation while Young Jones felt like he was drowning. She sat next to him on the bed and put her hand on his knee.

'Hi Babe, my name's Holly.'

'I'm Ben but everyone calls me Jonesy,' he blurted out. He was sure he must be blushing.

Holly held his hand ever so gently. The warmth expressing a tenderness that might not have been faked by a professional but may just have been genuine.

'It's okay Ben, there's no need to be nervous, I'm here to help you relax. Do you want to spend some time with me, Ben?'

Jonesy nodded urgently and said 'yes' so fast he almost stumbled over the simple word. She told him a price and he didn't hesitate to pull out his wallet and give her the money. She smiled at him.

'I'll just go put this away and then we'll begin. If you want you can take off your uniform and boots and relax a little, okay?'

She closed the door behind her. Young Jonesy wondered what he should do, he didn't feel comfortable just stripping off and waiting for her starkers but he felt silly to be still in uniform while she was expecting him to get undressed. So he stripped to his boxers and sat on the bed. She hadn't mentioned the ten percent discount for men in uniform. It was probably just automatically deducted or something, he thought.

Holly opened the door, all smiles and blonde hair.

'You can take off your boxers, it's alright, you won't need them just now.'

She smiled and removed the flimsy silky thing she was wearing revealing her naked body. This was the first he'd ever seen.

All doubt left his mind.

She lay down on the bed lazily reclining on her side like a graceful yet dangerous lady panther. Jonesy froze, what do you do with a hooker? He stared at her naked body.

'This is your first time, isn't it?'

Jonesy nodded.

'It's okay, I don't bite, just follow me.' She took his hand and put it on her breast. Jonesy was hers from that point on.

In the end the whole event from foreplay to conclusion took a grand total of fifteen minutes and forty seven seconds. Not that Jonesy was watching the clock or anything.

So that's it, he thought as he lay back in sweaty post coital bliss. I'm no longer a virgin. I'm a man now.

Holly lay on her side gently stroking his chest and smiling.

'Feeling good babe?' Jonesy nodded, the mousey grin of the happily deflowered on his face. Holly sat up.

'I want to try on your hat,' she announced, leaning over his naked body to reach his hat. Her belly brushed over his flaccid and startled penis while she leant over him.

Lying next to him again, she examined the black cap with HMAS Parramatta written across the front. She gently put it on her own head. The locks of her blonde hair stuck out the sides and the back. She looked like a little girl who has found something belonging to a grown up and tried it on.

'Ahoy there mateys!' she said in a silly pirate accent.

Jonesy smiled. 'We're the Navy, not pirates.'

'Well, what do you say in the Navy then?'

'Things like "man the rails" or "all hands battle stations" You know, military stuff.'

She cocked the hat and tried again.

'All hands battle stations,' she said and performed a mock salute, naked except for his hat, her breasts on display, the finest and only pair Young Jonesy had ever seen. She leaned down and rested herself on his chest, his hat still on her head.

'Do you like being in the Navy?'

'Not really, it's not what I expected or hoped it would be. I kind of think I might have made a mistake.'

'What did you think it would be?'

He shrugged, unsure of how to explain himself.

'I don't know, something noble or heroic or worthwhile. So far all I've done is training and cleaning. It all seems a bit pointless and not worth the bother to me. I think I should have gone to university or something instead.'

'I'm doing uni at the moment, it's pretty good but I'll be glad when it's over and I can go do what I want to do.'

'What degree are you doing?'

'Agricultural Science.'

He nodded. The idea that this woman had a life outside this place hadn't really registered. Of course she did, he thought now, she was someone's daughter, someone's sister, someone's friend, and she had taken money from him so that he could lose his virginity finally.

'Do you want to have a quick shower before you go?'

He nodded and stood up.

When he was showered and dressed she kissed him and led him back to the waiting room. Smithy walked into the room at the same time.

'How'd you go young fella? Shoot yer custard did ya? She make a man out of you or what?'

His loud, boisterous voice grating. Jones felt he'd like to punch Smithy in the face one day. Or at least tell him what a fuckwit he was. Tell him right to his face that he despised him and hoped to never become anything like him.

Smithy was in a good mood as they walked down the street in the Fremantle sunshine.

'This is living, Young Jonesy, a man can make a grand old life of things if he knows what's what, I tell you what.'

Jonesy wondered what his parents were doing now. He thought about the Gawler Baptist Church and the many happy years he'd had growing up in and around its old stone walls. He thought about Holly and what she was doing now. Would another man have gone with her by now? Would she remember him at all in a week's time?

Smithy led them to the Norfolk Hotel which had a large beer garden facing towards the main road. A bunch of the other blokes from the ship were there, already several beers into it.

'C'mon Young Jonesy, you need a refreshing ale or three after your debut performance today.'

They joined the other men from the ship around a big table in the corner. Smithy called for their attention as the beers arrived.

'Now we have a special reason to drink up today. Young Jonesy here has popped his cherry today, that's right, he's a man now.'

The sailors all roared with laughter and cheered.

'ONYA JONESY!'

'SHOT YA CUSTARD, OLD MATE!'

'WATCH OUT NOW, LADIES. JONESY'S GOT A TASTE FOR IT!'

The laughter and the shouting made him blush which only encouraged them to laugh and shout more. A beer was pressed into his hand with shouts of 'Get it down ya!' and he was made to skull it. More beer flowed. Someone asked how much time they had before they had to be back on ship.

'A solid four hours until we have to be back on the Good Ship Lollipop, so drink up mate!' Smithy assured them.

Jonesy, no longer the centre of attention, sat off to the side. He thought of his parents, the church which had been the centre of his life growing up. He thought of the twenty years his parents had spent in Sri Lanka. He thought of Holly again, the shape of her breasts and how she'd looked with his hat on and nothing else.

He thought of that passage of scripture his father liked to quote: "For what is seen is transitory, but what is unseen is eternal." And he looked around the beer garden.

At the other Navy men, at the locals, at the pretty girls dressed up for their day out, at the young bucks in suits dressed to impress, all of them drinking and talking and laughing. All of them alive for the moment, and for the moment only.

KEVIN BRADFIELD'S LEGACY

It was the day before Australia Day in 2023 when I received the letter. I was checking my mail at the Post Office. I had done a bit of online impulse shopping a few weeks before and I was expecting some books, a T-shirt and a couple of records from various websites, nothing major. Rather predictably they weren't there yet. Australia Post just isn't what it used to be. Instead, there was a letter from the Western Australia Department of Corrections.

What the fuck were they doing sending me a letter? I hadn't lived in WA for nearly twenty years at that point. Had I forgotten some petty fine or summons from back in the day? Some forgotten misdeed in my misspent youth that a computer somewhere had found buried in a file and now I would have to face court in Perth and maybe even do a little time?

It was from someone in the office who handled paroles for prisoners. It reminded me that I had testified regarding the murder of Kevin Bradfield back in November 2002. Two men, Thomas McEwan and Jason Small, had pleaded guilty to his murder and received a sentence of twenty years to life. They were up for parole now and as a concerned party (that's a strange phrase, I thought) I had the right to be consulted and give my statement at their parole hearing.

Well, fuck me, I thought, there's a blast — nay, a punch in the guts — from the past.

I had met Kevin in the Narcotics Anonymous meetings we both attended in Perth. I was about 21 at the time. We were both struggling to get our lives together with varying degrees of success, but Kevin was having less success than I was. He had lived rough all his life and it showed on his face. Despite only being five years or so older than me, he looked like he was forty at least. Life had been hard for him from the get-go and it had left scars.

He had a hole in his throat, the legacy of an emergency tracheotomy performed by an ambulance paramedic that had saved his life during one of his dozen or so near fatal overdoses. Despite, or perhaps because of this disfigurement he never bothered to quit smoking. He would talk to you by putting his finger on the hole and producing that raspy voice that was understandable if somewhat disconcerting, then casually put his cigarette in the hole and inhale deeply and with obvious pleasure. It took a little getting used to.

He told me a little bit about his life as I got to know him. His family had been poor white trash moving from crappy wheatbelt town to crappy wheatbelt town so his alcoholic itinerant labourer father could find work. His mother had been only semi-literate but basically kind. Kevin insisted to me, perhaps a little too much, that his family hadn't been unhappy. His father was a drunk but a jolly one, he said, and his mother might have been barefoot and pregnant most of the time but she was kind and loved her children. Kevin insisted that he didn't feel sorry for himself because of his poverty-stricken, semi-nomadic childhood.

He told me that he had actually been born in the Katanning caravan park. His mother had gone into labour and by the time the ambulance had been called his entry into the world had already happened. I don't know if that story was true but it would fit everything I know about his life.

Kevin's schooling was patchy at best. Moving from town to town, his father needing to follow the contracts and jobs to keep them fed, Kevin went to a string of small schools in small country towns, none of them very good. Instead of fitting in with the kids at every new school, he and his many siblings tended to band together and look after each other.

What Kevin really learned at school is that society is cold and indifferent to you if you're poor white trash. The teachers didn't care that much and didn't put much effort into teaching a poor labourer's kid who they knew would be moving on soon anyway. The town kids at school didn't like him and didn't include him. He began to understand that his family's poverty and rootlessness meant they would always be on the outer. Society had no real place for them, there would be no welcoming arms, no inclusion and no helping hand in hard times.

This was a hard understanding for a child to come to but it was probably accurate. Nobody cares about poor white trash kids in country towns. They're not a trendy cause, there is no movement for them; they're on their own. Ironically, Kevin would have been better off being born a refugee; someone might have cared about him then.

Kevin finished school as soon as he could. His choices in life were pretty limited. He worked with his dad labouring on farms and in an abattoir for a year or two. Deciding the life of a country working man was not for him, he headed for the city.

He hit Perth just as the big heroin wave of the '90s was getting underway. He'd already had experience with alcohol and weed in the country and he knew of speed as a truckie's drug but heroin was an unknown, exotic thing to a country boy like him.

He was working as a labourer on building sites and living in a doss house in Vic Park when he started using smack. Pretty soon the job went but he'd learnt to be resourceful as a poor kid in the country and had no qualms about breaking the law so he always found ways to fund his habit. He got arrested and did small amounts of time behind bars for petty things: possession, breaking and entering, trying to sell stolen goods. Prison was no great hardship to him. He'd spent a great deal of his youth living in caravan parks and temporary accommodation in the wheatbelt, so it didn't bother him much.

He got clean once or twice but it never stuck. The lure of the life was always too strong and looking back now, with the benefit of years and wisdom, I wonder if life clean really had all that much to offer him. Sure, being clean meant not going to prison and not hanging out for a shot but what else did it offer? Working a crappy labouring job and living on the bottom rung of the class ladder? Perhaps he simply weighed up the benefits of being clean and found them wanting. If you want people to aspire to the future you actually need to have a decent future to offer them. The world offered Kevin nothing.

Kevin wasn't stupid. A lot of people make the mistake of equating lack of education with lack of brains but they are not the same thing. Kevin was a sharp observer of the world and life and he thought things through as well as anyone. He was quite capable of seeing how the world worked and what his place in it was. There wasn't much fooling him.

I met him in early 2001 at an NA meeting in Perth. I liked him straight away; he was funny the way he'd talk in meetings and tell yarns about his misadventures. I think these escapades were what motivated him to try staying clean again. The heroin scene inevitably gets ugly and Kevin had been a small time dealer to fund his own habit. This led to his being robbed and bashed several times as well as having dealings with very heavy people higher up the drug chain. There are only so many beatings a man will take before he decides to re-think his life.

I remember sitting on the steps with him outside the State Library one afternoon. We'd been to the Hare Krishna joint which at the time was just around the corner. You could get a good feed of their veggie curry stuff for a gold coin donation back then. It probably kept a lot of people from starving and certainly was the only way I ate any veggies at the time.

I remember it was a sunny afternoon; the light streamed down through James Street and onto the steps where we sat. We ate fast, hoovering the food into our hungry mouths with no regard to formalities or table manners. We finished eating and sat there for a few moments watching the people come and go. We both got our smokes out and lit up for a post-dinner nicotine hit and then Kevin started telling me his story.

'So about two months ago I was sitting at home – this is when I still had the place in Carlisle near the train station. Anyway, I was sick and hanging out due to a lack of funds and whatnot when all of a sudden someone starts booting at the door.'

He paused his narrative to stick his cigarette in the hole in his throat and inhale like his life depended on it.

'You know how you can tell the difference between a regular knock on the door and someone trying to smash the door in? Well, this was definitely someone trying to smash the door in. All I could think at the time was "I fucking hope that's the cops" but of course it wasn't. Some retard had gone around telling every junkie south of the river that "Kevin's got lots of money and drugs" so of course these blackfellas decide to come and boot my door down for money and drugs that I just don't fucking have!'

'Long story short, they boot in the door and then start booting in my head, demanding I produce the drugs and money they've heard that I have. I told them, "Cunt, look around, does it look like I've got money or drugs." The dumb fucks have to stop and look at the fucking squalor I'm living in to realise I'm as broke as they are.'

'The biggest of the two realises they've wasted their time, kicks me in the ribs once more for good luck and calls me a "fucking pov cunt" as they walk out the door they've just booted off the hinges.'

He took another deep drag on his smoke.

'To add insult to injury, the landlady kicked me out, said I was bringing a bad element around and I wouldn't get my bond back because of all the damage.'

We sat and watched the sunshine bathe the city in healing light. Eventually I decided to say what was on my mind.

'Yeah man, that sort of shit is why I'm clean and doing the meetings. Fuck living like that. Being clean is hard sometimes but at least you don't have that nonsense on a regular basis.'

Being only twenty-one at the time I thought this was a profoundly intelligent and appropriate thing to say. Kevin didn't totally agree.

'Yeah, but y'know …' he began, finger on his tracheotomy hole, 'life goes so slow when you're clean, there's just so much boredom in life when you're off the smack.'

This sounded almost heretical to me at the time. I wasn't quite sure how to respond.

Later that night on the train home to Fremantle, I thought about what he'd said. I couldn't accept Kevin's point of view. To me life was something to be fought for. At some point in my addiction I'd seen where it was going. I'd had friends die; I knew what was likely to happen if I continued. I made a choice that I wanted to live and get more out of life than the junkie existence I was living. I saw how many people went under and I decided I wasn't going to be one of them. I was going to find a way out.

The NA meetings and staying clean was just the outward expression of this internal decision. The decision to live came first, then I found the way to make that work.

The idea that Kevin might decide not to live bothered me. The reasons he gave for maybe leaving the door open to future heroin use seemed really weak to me. It made me angry.

But I found I couldn't stay angry at Kevin. He was a genuinely funny bastard. A real ratbag with a heart of gold. I don't think I ever saw him express genuine malice or hostility to anyone. And the stories he'd tell! If ever there was a case of wasted talent, it was Kevin. He ought to have found a way to write down his stories and publish them like Chopper Reed did. His yarns were better than Chopper's, if you ask me. It's a crying shame that lack of education and drug addiction robbed the world of Kevin's story telling ability.

Through the period 2001-2002 I saw Kevin fairly regularly at NA meetings and around Perth. He'd sometimes go back to using for a few months and I think he did a short stint in jail during that time but he always returned to the meetings. I think, despite what he might have said, he wanted to stay clean and get his life into some sort of order.

The last time I saw Kevin was also the reason for the letter from the WA Corrections people.

Kevin had gone back using for a while. It was unfortunate but that was life in recovery. On the day in question, I had been idly wandering around the city thinking about my life and what I was going to do with it. I used to do this quite often.

Anyway, I'd wound up near the Royal Perth Hospital and it was nearly lunch time. I decided to head to the lunchtime NA meeting up in Highgate, so I started walking. I cut across Victoria Square where the Cathedral is and I spotted Kevin lurking just outside the emergency room of the hospital. He saw me and waved so I figured it couldn't be anything too dramatic.

'What's the good word, Kev?' I called out and he smiled back.

'Ah you know, just had to use the phone to talk to a man about a dog.'

He indicated the public phones outside the emergency room. I understood. He had to talk to his dealer, presumably he was dealing small time himself to fund his own habit and he had called his man, one rung up the food chain, to get a resupply.

I didn't judge him. I was a tiny bit disappointed but I genuinely liked Kevin and wished he'd stay clean for his own sake but I didn't want to lecture him or shut him out. There was some real affection in my heart for the man.

I told him, as nonchalantly as I could, that I was going to the lunchtime meeting. He nodded and paused a few minutes before speaking. Slowly, almost cautiously, he lifted his finger to the hole in his throat and said gently what was on his mind.

'Yeah, I'm gonna get back to it soon. I'm getting tired of the life, you know what I mean? Might be time I hung up my boots for good as far as smack goes, anyway.'

I was convinced he was genuine at the time and it gave me a warm feeling in my heart. Maybe we were all going to be alright after all.

I wished him well and we parted company.

I didn't pay any attention at the time but Kevin was being followed. About half an hour after that conversation, he was dead.

Two junkie pieces of shit, the previously mentioned Thomas McEwan and Jason Small, had been following Kevin, waiting for a chance to rob him of his cash and drugs. They knew he was calling his dealer on the public phones so they figured he must have cash on him. They waited until he went into a public toilet then ambushed him. They each had a cheap steak knife and they stabbed him multiple times in each side of his abdomen. Several arteries were cut and his lungs were punctured. He bled to death in the urinal of a grotty public toilet in East Perth near the McIver train station.

He had $1800 on him.

His killers took this money and put it up their arms within 48 hours. They were morons and kept their knives; they didn't change out of their blood splattered clothes either. Scoring heroin comes before hiding the evidence of a murder for a junkie. They were caught and it was a slam dunk case for the prosecution.

When I heard about it I went to the police and told them what I'd seen. Admittedly it wasn't much but it was sort of useful in helping the police establish a timeline for the events. I was prepared to testify in court but the early guilty plea of the killers meant I didn't have to.

They got life with a non-parole period of twenty years.

Hence the strange letter in the mail all these years later.

As I read it and thought about what it said it didn't seem real. That life I'd lived, those people I'd known, it may as well have been a hundred years ago for all the relevance it had to me now.

For lack of a better idea, I rang the phone number written in the letter. I was put through to a ridiculously young sounding woman full of professional courtesy and enthusiasm. Was this girl even born when Kevin died? I thought to myself. Did she understand the life that Kevin and I had lived back then?

I told her who I was and what I was ringing about. She told me about the upcoming parole hearing and what would be involved.

'I have to ask also, is there anyone else who might have a stake in this case? We are having trouble finding any family for Mr Bradfield. Do you have any idea?'

'I only know what he told me about his family, poor people who moved around a lot for work, mostly in the wheatbelt,' I said. 'Can't you find them? You found me. Actually, how did you find me?'

'You're on the electoral roll, it doesn't seem like any of Mr Bradfield's family is on the electoral roll. His ashes were claimed by his mother in 2002 but she doesn't seem to live at the address she gave back then. It's as though his family all died out or never existed. I've never seen anything like it. We're drawing total blanks. You're the only interested party we've been able to find.'

The cold enormity hit me. Kevin had been dead for just over twenty years and it was as though he'd been completely erased from existence. As though he'd never been alive in the first place.

What had happened to his family? Presumably most of them were dead as well but surely there would be someone who gave a fuck about this case? I couldn't be the sole surviving person who remembered Kevin Bradfield had once been alive.

Apparently I was the only person to carry a torch for the life and soul of one Kevin Bradfield who had been born in the Katanning caravan park and who died in a public toilet in East Perth.

Feeling a bit overwhelmed, I asked the young woman on the phone what would I have to do.

'Well, I can send you an email with some information about the offenders, their rehabilitation work and that sort of thing and then you can write a statement if you want about the impact Kevin's murder had on you and what you would like to see happen. The parole board takes all of this into consideration when it makes its decision.'

That seemed a reasonable way to proceed so I gave her my email address and she promised to send me the information later that day.

I waited until I had a full weekend to read it all.

Thomas McEwan had made good use of his twenty years in prison. He'd done his Year 12 certificate and passed. He'd completed training courses in welding and carpentry and worked in the prison workshop where they made playground equipment for disadvantaged Aboriginal communities. He had, by all reports, been a model prisoner and turned his life around. Several prison officers were apparently happy to go on record that he was rehabilitated and ready to re-enter society.

Jason Small had found Jesus in a big way. He had completed a correspondence course in ministry and counselling via Perth Bible College, an institution I had no idea existed. He led worship services in the prison and was a mentor of sorts to many troubled young men in the place. Again, several prison officers were happy to go on record saying he had been rehabilitated and was ready to re-enter society.

I stopped reading. What was I supposed to make of this? The absurdity of it all hit me. I'd known Kevin for about two years via Narcotics Anonymous meetings and now I was being asked to contribute to deciding if the men who'd murdered him were ready to leave prison and participate in life again.

A thought occurred to me as I looked through the documents she'd sent me. Jason Small had been 24 in 2002 and Thomas McEwan had been 26. That meant they'd be 44 and 46 respectively. That was a lot of life missed out on. The file said nothing about family, no wife or kids on the outside waiting for them. What sort of life would they be able to build for themselves if they got out? Would they be able to have a family? What woman would want to marry a former prisoner in his forties who did twenty years for murder?

I thought about my own life and what I'd been able to do with it in the twenty years since that time. I had a family, a job, one or two friends. I hadn't set the world on fire but I'd carved out my little slice of happiness. That's more than Kevin got. It was more than these two got either, twenty years in a cage. Maybe it would have been kinder to hang them.

The more I thought about it, the more I couldn't bring myself to demand blood. I couldn't bring myself to write back and demand they stay in their cage any longer. Kevin was dead. Kevin was apparently forgotten by everyone except me. Time had erased him.

Fuck it, I thought, there's no point.

I wrote an email back saying that I had no objection to the offenders being granted parole.

SUNDAY MASS
IN SMOKY BAY

Patricia woke just before the sun peeked over the horizon. She lay there silent and unmoving as the first rays of light illuminated the Bay.

She got up, careful not to wake Charles beside her, and pottered downstairs, the toilet first, then the kitchen for a cuppa, the standard morning ritual of an old person. When Charles got up he would turn the radio on and listen to the ABC News. Patricia hated it, utterly sick of that calm, sterile voice telling them passively of the world's woes while Charles sipped his tea. She found a gentle happiness in the silence of the morning and was increasingly reluctant to give it up when Charles woke up. This hour or so before he clambered downstairs was her time and precious to her.

She opened the curtains and looked out at the dawn sea. The house was built with as much ocean view as possible and a simple flicking open of the lounge room curtains gave her a panorama of the Bay that was worth a fortune. They, or rather Charles, had bought the block of land and built this house after they retired. Charles had painted her a picture of joyful, active retirement; fishing, socializing, grandkids visiting them on school holidays, it had sounded good. In fairness Charles had tried to stick with that plan. But somehow, somewhere along the way, they'd sunk into a rut.

Charles had felt the end of his working life like a man losing a limb. Turned out there wasn't much to him once you took away the getting up and going into the office every day. Since then he had shrivelled right before Patricia's eyes. Like a retired stud horse or sheep dog there didn't seem to be much point to his existence now.

He'd become increasingly enslaved to routine. His morning paper, his morning walk along the beach, listening to the same programs on ABC radio at the same times every day, grimly hanging on.

The grandkids visited on school holidays and gave them a respite from each other, injecting life into the house, but when they left it was quiet again and routine took over.

They hadn't made any friends locally, either. The Smoky Bay locals had their own lives and wealthy retirees who pushed up the real estate prices were resented. The small row of new houses where they lived were all inhabited by retirees from the city. They all had great views across the bay. They were all worth a lot of money. None of the elderly couples living in them spoke much with the others.

Patricia stared out the windows and watched a fishing boat head out of the Bay towards the open sea. It was a nice view but was it nice enough to justify forty years of her life? She sipped her tea and felt the immense weight of forty years gone by.

She heard Charles wake up. He made such a production that the entire house echoed to his stretching and yawning. God forbid if anyone else had wanted to sleep in. He stumbled downstairs, gave Patricia a perfunctory "Morning love" before flicking the kettle and the radio on. Patricia's spirit sank as the voice of the ABC presenter broke the silence.

Charles made his cuppa and sat down next to her.

'I'm going to Mass this morning,' she said.

Charles raised an eyebrow.

'Well, I'll walk with you then and keep going to the shop. I want to get *The Weekend Australian* and I may as well get some bread and milk while I'm down there.'

The Smoky Bay Community Church didn't look much from the outside. It was a shared church, each denomination, Catholic, Anglican and Lutheran, taking turns to hold their services on revolving Sundays. Smoky Bay wasn't big enough for each denomination to have their own church. The building was small and made of fibro; when the strong winds hit it, it would make creaking noises like a haunted house. No grand cathedral, yet Patricia was fond of it. She liked coming to Mass here. She'd been a sporadic attendee most of her adult life but since moving to Smoky Bay she'd become a regular and devoted communicant.

Charles left her outside the church with a casual 'Enjoy yourself love' and kept on walking towards the shop. Patricia entered the tiny church. She genuflected and crossed herself as she'd been doing since she was a girl. For a second she remembered her girlhood reverence, fear almost, of the big brick Church they'd attended. How impressive it had seemed back then. How thunderous had the priest's voice sounded, how vivid and dramatic the pictures of the Saints and Christ's Passion that lined the walls. But girlhood had given way to adulthood and marriage to Charles. Somewhere in that transition to adult life her faith had become a smaller thing, not as important, to be done if there was time and energy, after paying the mortgage and getting the kids into a good school. From wondering at the stories of the Saints to calculating mortgage payments and school catchment areas, a fitting metaphor for growing up.

There were a few minutes left before the scheduled start of the service. Patricia sat down on a pew in the middle row and looked around her. It wasn't a big crowd; the people of Smoky Bay didn't feel much need for religion. There was a family and a young woman and that was it.

Patricia had seen the family before. Regulars, the father looked to her like a farmer, hard and wind-blasted from a lifetime spent in paddocks. His wife looked pleasant enough, small but dignified with a full head of raven hair that caught the light like the ceremonial garb of an ancient pagan priestess. They had a healthy brood of children. Patricia counted six but wouldn't be surprised if more came along later. It seemed the old stereotypes about Catholics had some basis in reality still.

The young woman was a mystery. She was scruffy, slightly hippy-looking, as if she'd been living out of the back of a van for a while. Patricia had actually seen her arrive in town a few months earlier. She'd been at the General Store when the Premier Stateliner Bus had arrived and this young woman had stepped off along with a couple of other people. Patricia had paid her no attention at the time, assuming she was just another backpacker passing through town. She'd seen her at the Caravan Park and presumed she'd gained a job there for the season. Then she'd started attending Mass. Patricia wondered who she was and where she'd come from.

The Priest began the service, his robes catching the light as the wind rattled the fibro walls of the church. He blessed them and spoke of the blessing of the lord on this little church with its tiny congregation.

One of the Farmer's daughters read the scripture, it was the second half of Matthew chapter 19, the parable of the rich man. Patricia heard the line about the rich young man who "went away sad because he had many possessions" and Christ's warning about the temptations of worldly wealth. A great sadness descended on her as the scripture was read.

The Priest gave a homily centred around the reading. He said the real meaning of life was to walk lightly through this world as a pilgrim, he suggested, even as a refugee, our real destination and home being the kingdom of God. No real happiness was possible, he asserted, in this temporary world full of sin, cruelty and death. Don't be like the rich young man in the scripture today, he exhorted, rejecting Christ and ultimate joy for mere worldly possessions.

The ritual of the Mass began. 'Blessed are you Lord God of all creation, through your goodness we have this bread to offer.' The words washed over Patricia, soothingly pleasurable. The host was raised and blessed, the wine was raised and blessed. Solemnly the tiny congregation formed a line in front of the rough alter. Pilgrims, refugees even, from the cruel world outside, gathered here in this little fibro church to partake of the miracle and hope for ultimate joy.

Patricia was at the end of the small line but it didn't bother her. For those few moments she was full of joy and wonder. A miracle was occurring here in this little church, she assured herself, life wasn't just a drudgery of paying bills, raising children and putting up with Charles. Life was a pilgrimage to joy, she was certain of this, at least she wanted to be certain of this.

The Priest spoke to end the service. 'Go now to love and serve the Lord in peace'. And the tiny congregation began to file out of the Church. The wind was up and the young woman's long hair flicked about, making it impossible for Patricia to see her face. Patricia slowly walked back to the house, the warm and pleasant thrill of religious devotion gradually fading with each step she took.

Charles was settled into his chair at the kitchen table with *The Weekend Australian* spread out before him.

'Tell you what, dear. If Labor win the next election we're all going to be ruined, these taxes they want to bring in will send everyone to the wall, it's madness!'

Patricia stifled an urge to scream. If she was lucky she could have a nap for an hour or so in the afternoon and sleep away some of the time left to her in this life.

She looked out the lounge room windows at the expensive view of the Bay.

AS FAR AS CULTANA

She was awake when he got up to get ready for work but lay still pretending to be asleep. She heard him wolf down some toast, have a shower and get dressed. Rain was still falling in fits and starts, a percussion ensemble on the tin roof.

He walked back into the bedroom just before he left. He looked her over as she lay there faking sleep. For a second she thought he would say something; then he leaned over and kissed her on the side of her face before leaving. He'd kissed her on the side that was still faintly bruised; there was a slight stinging sensation as his stubble and lips touched the tender skin and it took a lot of effort for her not to wince.

She heard his car start and ease out of the driveway. She lay in bed for a few minutes to make sure he didn't come back then she got out of bed.

She had played out this morning in her head for months.

The money was stashed in an old Milo tin at the very back of the cupboard. She pulled it out and counted it again, four hundred and seventy-five dollars and fifty cents, enough to get her to Adelaide and keep her going for a couple of days while she looked for a job or something. She stuffed half in her purse and the other half in her bag of clothes hidden underneath her socks and underwear.

She wasn't taking much, two bags of clothes and a few little things, not enough to half fill the boot of the car. The car itself she viewed as a possible source of income if she was tight for money once she reached Adelaide. It was only two years old; she could get a bit of money for it and Adelaide had public transport, so it wasn't such a big deal to be without a car.

Feeling as ready as she was ever going to be she took her bags outside and put them in the car. This was a moment she feared: what if he came back while she was halfway through putting the bags in the car? She shivered at the thought.

She loaded everything in the car and locked the front door. For a moment her courage deserted her and she wanted to cry that this had all been a big mistake, a momentary tantrum that she now repented. She breathed in and out slowly. She found her courage again, slid in the driver's seat, buckled up, and turned the key.

The rain stopped as she drove out of Port Lincoln. The green, sodden paddocks passed outside the car window as she drove with the heater on and the radio down low. She passed North Shields and Louth Bay in a state of numbness.

Somewhere near the turn off for Tumby Bay the rain started again. A miserable dripping that splattered her windscreen like piss from on high. The heater struggled to keep the windscreen free of fog. The noise of it annoyed her so she turned up the radio. The Port Lincoln station she normally listened to faded out of range so she searched through the dial for something. She found a golden oldies station on the AM dial eventually and listened to Glen Campbell singing about being a Wichita Lineman.

The rain continued as she drove past the turn offs for Port Neil and Arno Bay, the golden oldies station played some Dusty Springfield as she drew closer to Cowell.

She'd left Port Lincoln with a full tank and probably only needed to top up once, maybe twice on the way to Adelaide.

Was it better to top up in Cowell or to wait until she got to Port Augusta?

The rain had eased a little by the time she stopped at the bowser. The cold hit her as she stepped out of the car and she shivered a little while she pumped fuel. She slid the money across the counter.

'Is it alright if I leave the car there for a minute while I use the toilet?' she asked.

'Hardly anyone on the road today with this awful weather,' the old lady with the missing teeth in her smile reassured her. 'Reckon you'll be alright, love.'

As she sat on the toilet she took her phone out. Fingers numb with cold she unlocked her phone and there it was.

'Got home from work early, where are you?'

He knew. Or if he didn't know he was going to work it out soon enough when she didn't come home.

Her flickering flame of courage was no match for the cold roadhouse toilet and the words on her phone.

She swallowed hard.

Back on the highway heading north, she felt a little stronger as she increased the distance between them. Just keep driving, she told herself, just keep driving.

The rain continued as she drove towards Whyalla, a solid wall of wet and misery following her up the Spencer Gulf. The golden oldies station played some Joni Mitchell and that one Beatles song she liked. By the time she arrived at Whyalla she listened half-heartedly to the radio news. Some kids on the main street gave her the finger for no apparent reason. She kept driving. If I had to grow up in Whyalla I'd be angry at the world too, she thought.

She had cleared Whyalla entirely and Cultana was on her left side now. The fences with the little signs regularly spaced informing you this was Department of Defence property and there was live ammunition being used here, were visible now. She couldn't see any of the Army people or their vehicles there, so maybe they weren't doing exercises right now? She pulled into the first rest area she saw.

The rain eased up a little as she sat and cried in the car. She stepped out of the car and walked around the rest area. She was still crying when the phone rang. It was him.

'Darling, where are you at?'

It was a minute before she could speak.

'I'm on the road, in a rest area, just near Cultana.'

'And why are you all the way up there, my darling?'

He sounded reptilian and mocking.

'I'm … I'm … I'm leaving you.'

He laughed a short laugh that could have been fake but might not have been.

'Oh, don't be silly my darling, turn around and come home, it's much too cold and wet for this nonsense. I'll get us Chinese for dinner tonight and we can take it easy, ok?'

He projected such confidence and assurance. She cried the last of her tears and spoke quietly into the phone.

'Okay, I'll come home.'

He hung up. She stood alone in the rest area for a few moments.

Well, she thought as her tears became one with the rain, I made it as far as Cultana this time. Starting the car again, she turned around for home.

CAREER ADVICE FROM AN OLD SAILOR

I was probably born with the love of telling and hearing stories. I have been doing it as long as I can remember. The impulse to tell a cracking good yarn, and not let the truth get in the way of said yarn, has always been with me.

When I was young the older generations I grew up around were not only great story tellers but they had plenty of material for their yarns. The generation who lived through the Second World War was still alive back then and some of them would tell you about their experiences after a couple of tinnies.

There was also the generation of Aussie blokes who'd fought in the Asian Wars, Korea, Malaya, Borneo and Vietnam, and they could tell a yarn or two. Some of them, after a few more beers, would tell the most off-tap, outrageous yet hilarious stories about prostitutes in the countries where they'd fought. I got the impression that there were more casualties from the Clap than there were from enemy action.

Living as I did in Western Australia there were plenty of Ten Pound Poms still around back then. The government had enticed British people to Australia in massive numbers with subsidised passages, ten pounds a head, and the dream of a better life. They were the parents and grandparents of the kids I went to school with. They'd come on their migrant ships in the '40s, '50s and '60s. The boat had docked at Fremantle, they'd had a look around and decided "this place looks alright" and never left WA after that. Entire suburbs of Perth back then were full of Ten Pound Poms and their descendants.

I used to hear some of these people telling yarns at family barbeques after a beer or two. I was fascinated with the country they'd come from and the history they'd seen. Some of them had survived the Blitz, seen German planes shot down and their pilots taken prisoner. Many of them had served in the British forces during the National Service era. One old bloke I remember had been in one of the last British regiments to leave India. He recalled vividly the ceremony where the Union Jack was taken down for the last time and the Indian flag flown for the first time.

It seems strange now, writing this in 2021 but recalling my memories from the 1980s and 1990s, how recent events like The Second World War and The British Empire seemed to me back then because of the influence of those old men. Things like the Normandy Landings and the Fall of Singapore were within living memory for thousands of people at that time. I hope someone recorded some of these people's memories for posterity.

I remember feeling that these epic events of history which these people had lived through were just beyond the horizon, just out of sight to the naked eye, and represented, in some way I couldn't explain at the time, a better, more heroic and meaningful world. In the way that young boys often do I dreamed of going to war and winning glory for myself, of being THERE when the big events happened that were written about in books. Instead, I was condemned to school followed by a lifetime of wage slavery and paying bills. Instead of the heroic older generation who had gone to wars and seen amazing things, I had the Baby Boomer Generation (as represented by my parents) who saw life as an endless struggle to pay bills and keep jobs.

The older generations had fought wars, seen the rise and fall of great powers and witnessed historical events of epoch-shaking importance. My parents' generation talked about mortgages and new furniture and the economy. From warriors to wage slaves, the decline of Western Civilization in a nutshell.

There was one old bloke, his name was Clive if I remember right. He was a Ten Pound Pom, the father of one of my school friends. He used to tell some cracking yarns once he got a couple beers in him at barbeques.

Clive was a Yorkshireman of the old-fashioned variety. Do you remember a TV show called "Heartbeat"? There was a character on that show called Claude Greengrass and I swear Clive spoke exactly like Claude Greengrass. Thick as fuck Yorkshire accent, almost impenetrable.

Clive had grown up in dismal poverty in some grim shithole in Yorkshire of the sort that George Orwell would have written about. There wasn't much of a future for a young lad in a place like that so at the ripe old age of 15, Clive went to sea in the merchant navy, working as a kitchen boy on a ship that moved freight back and forth across the Atlantic.

He adapted to the life of a merchant sailor very quickly and spent the next twenty years on one commercial ship or another sailing from port to port and drinking and whoring his way around the world. Clive would get a couple beers in him and be only too happy to tell me stories about his wild times at sea. Some of the stories were about things that happened at sea; hurricanes, huge sharks following the ship for days on end, that sort of thing. But get a couple more beers in him and Clive would tell the best stories. The drinking and whoring in ports around the world stories.

Looking back, I'm shocked but delighted that an only slightly tipsy adult would tell such tales to a young boy. We need more of that sort of thing in today's world, I think.

Clive had some weird fascination with women of colour. I don't know why. He would tell these elaborate tales of drunken misadventures in various ports and it would always end with him in a brothel with a woman from another race. He'd cap off the story in his thick Yorkshire accent like so:

"And then I went upstairs to Madam Tao's place and fooked me first Oriental Lass."

Or, "And then we made into Kingston, Jamaica and I went ashore and fooked me first Negro Lass."

Always like that.

I loved these stories and got the impression that a merchant sailor's life was one long drinking and whoring expedition around the world.

I was so enthralled by this idea I nearly became a merchant sailor myself.

At my shitty high school I was a class clown and trouble-maker. I had no interest in learning anything and despised the teachers, the system and just wanted out. They sent me to this guidance counsellor eventually, hoping in vain to straighten me out. The guidance counsellor asked me if there was any career or trade I might be interested in doing after school.

I told her the truth; that I wanted to avoid wage slavery and the horrible normality that I saw my parents living so was planning to either become a rock star, sell drugs or just go on the dole, possibly all three. Of course she didn't take me seriously. Why is it that when you tell the truth, teachers think you're talking shit? Anyway, she pushed me; there must be some sort of profession or trade or career I had an interest in?

I don't know why but Clive popped into my head at that moment, so I asked about becoming a merchant sailor on a commercial ship. What tickets would you have to get? How would you go about doing it?

The guidance counsellor was excited. I'd finally shown an interest in something productive. She tracked down the information with gusto. Remember this was in the pre-internet world so tracking down this info meant making phone calls, sending out letters and waiting for letters and brochures to arrive in the mail. She put in a lot of effort on my behalf, now that I think about it.

Eventually, she gave me a bunch of glossy brochures from something called the "Maritime Training College of Australia" or something like that. I was actually impressed and interested. The brochures outlined the courses available, what tickets they would result in and what jobs you could get with those tickets. They said nothing about the drinking and whoring around the world but I assumed they'd tell you that once you got on a ship.

For the first and last time in my school career I gave a shit and put in some effort. For a few weeks there I was actually a good student and had a goal to work towards.

Then I realised how happy the teachers were and how my parents seemed satisfied, like they'd won something. Well, I thought, this shit stops right now, and proceeded to undo everything. I went right back to wagging off school, being a class clown and a disruption. Fuckers thought I'd comply with their system, did they? Well, I'd show them. I amped up the misbehaviour and made my teachers' lives hell.

Several years after finishing (read: failing) high school I was broke, living in a doss house and had no career prospects at all.

Yeah, I sure fucking showed them.

THE ONLY TEACHER
WHO EVER REACHED ME

I knew her as Mrs Lechski but I later found out her first name was Janet. She was my English teacher in Year 9 at the shitty high school I attended unwillingly in Geraldton, the shithole town on the coast of Western Australia where I grew up.

I was not a good student. I was a class clown and a disruption, a vandal and an idle daydreamer. I had a deeply unhappy home life and as is often the case with kids, the abuse I suffered at home fuelled the trouble I caused at school. The beatings I received at home from my father transformed into vandalism and disruption at school.

My parents were religious nuts of the worst sort. Part of a grim Protestant sect which has since declined to the point where closing up shop is likely in the next few years. They had absorbed that fundamentalist mentality which teaches that life is a trial to be endured on behalf of a stern but loving God and one pleases this God most by cutting all joy, fun and laughter out of life.

My father in particular had really taken to a life based entirely on fear. Of his two fears, the two governing dooms of his life, the first was the economic fear. As Orwell once put it, "Thou shall not lose thy job." This fear haunted him constantly. He counted every penny and didn't hesitate to berate me if I happened to waste something for which he had paid.

'Do you have any idea what that cost?' he'd roar right in my face, his slab-like visage the very picture of enraged stupidity. I grew up with the knowledge that he was constantly frightened of losing his job and being unable to pay bills. I resolved as a young teenager to never be like him when I grew up. I resolved never to care about a job or worry about money, to never put any effort into work or careers and to cruise through life as much as possible. I am proud to say I have achieved this; I have never given a fuck about a job and I have still managed not to starve, so there you have it, kids!

The second governing fear of my father's life was religious. His Jehovah God was stern and wrathful and waited to smite sinners with eternal doom. Satan lurked about seeking to lure us all into sin and ruin. Only by cleaving to God's word and his unchanging moral standards could one avoid eternal damnation.

My father was constantly on the watch for sin and impurity entering his house and our lives. According to him, TV was Satan's tool for filling our minds with immoral sexual desires. Funny, but when I watched the shows that were popular at the time, cheesy sitcoms like *Full House* and *Family Matters*, all I was filled with was boredom.

The big vehicle of Satan's plans at the time was music. This was the early 90s and the alternative rock thing had happened in a big way. This was where the big separation between my father and me occurred. He wanted me to worship his Jehovah God. Instead I worshipped Kurt Cobain. He wanted me to believe in the Bible. I believed in Metallica and the Black Album. He put his faith in Jesus Christ. I put mine in Pearl Jam.

Music completely overtook my life from the time I first heard the *Nevermind* album. I didn't care about much else really. I spent what little money I had on tapes and music magazines. I obsessed about bands and scenes and albums in a way I have never obsessed about anything. I lived and breathed the glorious, anarchic, godless freedom hymn of that early 90s alternative rock. It was my religion. It was my liberation.

My father, of course was having none of this. He destroyed my tapes with a hammer and tore up my music magazines if he could find them. I became adept at hiding them and generally being an excellent little sneak. You'll often find kids who grew up in fundamentalist homes have these skills. Sneaking forbidden things is the only way to stay sane in that environment. On the bright side, if I am ever in some sort of prison camp or gulag I will already have the skillset to smuggle in contraband.

School was just an added misery on top of the misery of growing up fundamentalist. On the one hand my father distrusted the school system as an instrument of Satan's world. He'd especially get uppity about the teaching of evolution. 'They just make that stuff up,' he'd say, chin stuck out in pugnacious, wilful ignorance. 'Those fossils aren't real, it's just Satan's way of misleading people away from Jehovah.'

On the other hand, his economic fears made him think that if I didn't do well at school, I would be living under a bridge by the time I was 25. He'd constantly predict economic doom for my future. 'You'll be lucky to get a job flipping burgers if you don't buck up your attitude, boy.' I personally didn't care. I knew older kids in town who flipped burgers for a job and they were fun guys who always had beer and weed and were down to party and listen to rad tunes on their days off. This seemed a better life than my father's, to be honest.

Mrs Lechski stood out from the rest of the teachers at school because she actually cared. She gave a shit about teaching English and her students and honestly tried to make a difference. This was unusual at the time. Back in those days (it might still be like this, I don't know) the Teacher's Union was a powerful force. They had the ear of the State Government and a united membership which meant they basically got what they wanted whenever they wanted it. Essentially becoming a teacher in those days meant a guaranteed income until you retired or died, whichever came first. Unless you actually molested or bashed a student you couldn't be fired. Mere incompetence or laziness were no grounds for dismissal. As a result, the teaching profession tended to attract the dregs of the middle class. Mediocrities and white-collar bums, the sort of people who really had nothing to offer bright young minds with questions and ambitions.

I wonder now how many potentially high achieving young people were discouraged and stifled by the dismal quality of the teachers back then? How many future artists, scientists and other high achievers got the light inside them snuffed out by such small-minded middle-class nobodies and settled for a life consumed by slow decay? How many lives were downgraded, constricted and defeated before they even started, and for what? So a bunch of people from the lower end of the middle class could have a comfortable income and retirement benefits at the expense of the taxpayers? It outrages me when I think about it now.

Mrs Lechski had a passion for literature. She believed in books. She believed in art. She believed in their ability to change the world for the better. I remember her explaining it once; I can still recall everything she said to this day.

'Books do change the world; in fact, a good book is more likely to change the world than a politician because a good book is more powerful. Books get inside people's heads in a way that politicians can only dream of. Think for a moment of some famous books and the changes they brought. Think of *Oliver*

Twist. Before then nobody was much bothered about child labour and orphans but because of that book child labour laws were passed in every civilized country and we think differently about the subject than we did before. Think of *1984*, a book that has entered our very language and changed the way we think about government surveillance and truth. Or think of *The Bell Jar*, a book which changed the way we think about women's lives and mental health. All of these authors changed the world, not through the power of governments or armies but through the power of words written on a page. Never doubt the power of books.'

I remember the passion with which she spoke; I remember being actually impressed with a teacher for the first time ever.

I was a big reader. The local public library was a safe haven away from my father and also a source of forbidden knowledge. I was only too happy to spend my Saturday afternoon there. My reading was prolific but rather haphazard. With no plan or guide, basically if I found something at the library that looked interesting I gave it a go with no regard to genre or taste. Thus I happily flitted between *The Hitchhiker's Guide to Galaxy* series to a rather battered-looking copy of Henry Miller's *Tropic of Cancer* that I found half hidden behind other books in the library.

It was Mrs Lechski who first started ever so gently steering my reading in a concrete direction.

She had noted that I was a reader and a quiet thinker. She saw how I actually paid attention to what she said and decided to encourage me. One day she gave me a copy of *The Tin Drum* by Gunter Grass.

'I think you might get something from this Luke, it's about a boy who hides his true nature from everyone and observes what is really going on in the world around him. He gives us an insight into the way people followed the Nazis and …'

'Yeah, this is the book the Bronski Beat got their name from,' I interrupted her. She looked somewhat astonished.

'That's an odd little bit of information to know. How and why do you know that?'

'I read it in a music magazine,' I shrugged, slightly embarrassed to have shown what I knew.

She looked at me like I was deeper water than she had previously realised but she smiled, perhaps pleased as well as surprised.

'I don't think you read music magazines, I think you study them. I think you're dreaming of the day you get interviewed by one of them.'

The truth of her words cut through me. She had seen me naked in a sense. I was more than embarrassed now but she reassured me.

'It's okay; ambition is not a dirty word.'

She said no more and I took the book she had given me home, feeling like I had just had my guts exposed to someone in a far more intimate way than I was comfortable with.

Over the weekend I read *The Tin Drum* and loved it. Poor little Oscar, his urges to vandalism reflected my own. "Glass! all glass!" I smiled when I read that.

I even added a little literary flair to my vandalism as a result of reading the book.

I worked out how to make small holes in windows quietly using a thick towel, an egg ring and a ball peen hammer. Most of the time I didn't steal anything. I just liked to vandalise and destroy things, acting out from the abuse and misery at home.

So I started writing "Oscar!" in flowery handwriting above the little holes I made in shop and car windows. Not only was I getting the satisfaction of vandalising and destroying something but also the satisfaction of showing I was smarter and better read than the people in this shithole town. It made me feel good. The local police were probably looking for someone named Oscar, stupid fucks.

Mrs Lechski was the only person in town who got the reference. She pulled me aside after class and told me to stop with the vandalism. I lied right to her face and said I had no idea what she was talking about. She looked at me deadpan and said "Glass, all glass!" The exact same line from the book that had made me smile. My guilty blushing half-smile must have given me away. I mumbled some excuse, I don't remember what, and I never did that particular type of vandalism again.

Of all the sad memories of my youth the saddest is of April 1994, Kurt Cobain died of a self-inflicted shotgun blast and it felt to me like all light and hope had gone out of the world.

I was distraught, I was 14 years old and probably being a tad dramatic as 14-year-olds tend to be, but he had meant freedom, liberation and hope. To lose him, and in such a defeated way too, felt like the sun had ceased to shine.

The worst part of it was my arsehole father's reaction. He saw it on the news and turned to me with that smug, hateful sneer he had and said, 'Another one goes under; that's what you get for playing that bloody satanic music!'

If I'd had a gun at that moment I would have killed him. I don't think I've ever hated anyone so much before or since. I was, of course, powerless to do or say anything. Talking back would have resulted in yet another hiding for me.

I'm sober now, haven't had a drink in over a decade, but when my father finally dies, I think I'll make an exception and pop a bottle of something nice.

Of course, the misery I felt became fuel for more acting out at school and around town. More vandalism, more fighting, more back chatting teachers. Mrs Lechski noticed and unlike most teachers gave a fuck. She had also heard the news about Kurt Cobain. She saw my increased level of anti-social acting out and put two and two together.

'Luke, I know you're upset about Kurt's death but acting out the way you're doing is only going to make your life harder. I want you to channel what you're feeling. I want you to learn to control and focus your rage.'

'I'm going to assign you an essay to write, Luke, I want you to explain what Kurt Cobain meant to you personally. Don't worry about marks and don't worry about the other kids in class, this is just something you're going to show me personally and it'll be between us, ok?'

I nodded, unsure of myself. I still struggled with the idea of a teacher actually giving a shit about me. None of the other teachers cared, so why should this one? Somehow, almost against my better judgement, I trusted and believed in Mrs Lechski. I went home and wrote the essay.

It was by far the most passionate and eloquent thing I've ever written. I explained how Nirvana made me feel alive and free. How the ragged, jangly chords at the beginning of "Drain You" expressed the life bursting out of me, how the heavy main riff of "Lithium" expressed that same life being slowly crushed by the grim realities of the world around me. I explained how "Dumb" soothed the hurts of life while "Rape Me" focused the anger at how shitty the world was into window-smashing rage.

I explained how Nirvana had given me something that was intimately mine and at the same time collectively belonging to my generation. I explained how it felt to finally have someone who could speak for us, who was ours, who didn't belong to our parents. No more did we have to listen to our Baby Boomer parents waffle on about the Beatles or Bob Dylan. We had our own thing now and they couldn't understand it or touch it.

And, of course, I wrote down how it felt to lose all that. How Kurt's death felt like a defeat for all of us. I explained how there didn't seem to be much hope anymore, our little moment of rebellion and freedom felt like it had been snuffed out. Only the grim conformity of school and the workplace loomed on the horizon.

I wish I had kept that essay I wrote for her. In truth it was probably the best thing I have ever or will ever write.

I quietly gave it to Mrs Lechski after class, almost embarrassed that I'd actually written it. Like, actually caring about school, dude, what the fuck?

She read it all that night and pulled me aside the next day.

'Luke, that was wonderful, you made me feel and understand what you felt and that is no small achievement. You have real talent. Have you ever thought about becoming a writer?'

For a second, standing there with her in the otherwise empty class I felt something warm, beautiful and hopeful blossom inside me. This wonderful, intelligent woman had taken an interest in me and seen something, some potential to be more than a miserable wage slave like my arsehole father, some possibility of getting something more out of life than what a shithole like Geraldton had to offer. For a few seconds I saw a whole new path in life opening up in front of me.

Then the invincible negativity of an angry, damaged teenager won out.

'As if, you have to go to uni for that shit and I'll be fucked if I'm doing any more school than I legally have to. I'm finishing school the day I turn 16, signing on for the Youth Allowance dole and catching the bus to Perth. I'm gonna get a band started down there and I'm fucking never looking back at this shithole.'

I saw the hurt look on her face and it makes me cringe to look back on it now and realise what a shit I was to someone who was going out of her way to try and help me. I wish I could go back and undo that.

She talked a little more but no made progress with me that day. The angry, negative, hateful persona I wore like armour to protect myself from a cold and cruel world couldn't be breached by her.

She didn't give up though.

Unbeknownst, to me, she had called my parents and arranged to talk to them. They came in and sat opposite her. This intelligent, cultured and compassionate woman sat across a table from my slab-faced, brutal and moronic father and my small-minded fearful idiot of a mother. I wonder what she thought of them? I wonder if she realised, "Oh, this is why poor Luke is fucked up" as she looked at them?

She suggested to my parents that I attend some sort of extra-curricular camp in the school holidays. It was some sort of program for gifted English students. From what she told me about it later it sounded like it was designed to take the kids who were good at English and direct their talents into something creative and productive. It was loosely connected with the English program at UWA and most of the kids who went to the camp ended up going there after finishing Year 12.

Of course, my parents weren't having it.

'You think you're gonna go off and bludge at some fancy English book camp nonsense? You've got another think coming, boy!'

The predictable knuckle-dragging stupidity and aggression of my father was depressing but unsurprising.

'Why can't you be good at something that makes money? Can't be good at welding or carpentry, can you? No, have to be bloody good at bloody English book reading nonsense. Well, I've got news for you, boy. Nobody is going to pay you to read books! You'll be working at Hungry Jack's for the rest of your life if you don't get with it, boy!'

The economic argument spelled out, my father then turned to the religious case against it.

'And don't get me started about the worldly influences at something like that. Most of those books are unclean and filthy in the eyes of Jehovah. These bloody book writing types just put out scribbles about sex and drugs and all those people in the city praise it because they love their sin!'

He warmed up to his theme and got right up in my face, loud and aggressive, as he hammered home his point. His face like a slab of ham, but somehow stupider and louder, mere centimetres from my face in a fit of rage and indignation.

'All that arts stuff and those books that teacher wants you to read is part of Satan's world! That's what you're trying to be part of, is it? Whose side are you on? Jehovah's or Satan's? Because if you want to be part of that filthy world and write filthy books you can get out of this house right now.'

As I look back on these memories now all I can feel is pity for the boy I was and what I had to endure. That and hate, hate for my father, hate for his idiotic religion, hate for the useless cunts of teachers who didn't see the obvious signs of a boy suffering abuse at home and try and do something. Hate for a system that allowed me to fall through the cracks unnoticed and uncared about, hate for a cold and indifferent world that turns a blind eye to what kids suffer behind closed doors. Just hate, so much hate. I can't feel anything else about it.

A week or two later Mrs Lechski took me aside again.

'Your parents aren't keen on you going to the camp, are they, Luke?'

I'd copped another hiding from my father in the intervening time and I was in no mood for her help. The defensive negativity came out again.

'Can't you just fuck off and mind your own business? You're not helping, you're just making things worse.'

She was not dissuaded.

'Luke, this camp could really open doors for you and teach you all kinds of things. This is an opportunity to use your talent, you do have talent Luke, it just needs some direction and —'

'Just fuck off!' I interrupted, giving her both barrels of my rage. 'You think my family is like your family, don't you? You think I'm growing up in a nice middle-class home with nice middle-class parents who care, who encourage me? I wish! My parents are fucked in the head, this town is fucked and this school is fucked. Stop trying to push unrealistic dreams on me. I wasn't born lucky like you, I wasn't born into a nice middle-class home with nice parents who encourage me. I was born into this shit and it's fucked but I can't do anything about until I'm old enough to leave. I just want to bide my time as quietly as I can until I turn 16, then I can get the Youth Allowance dole and get out of here. So until then stop trying to help me, just fuck off and stop caring, like all the other teachers do.'

I was probably being a bit dramatic but I was honest. I knew the situation was hopeless. My parents weren't going to suddenly stop being arseholes. I wasn't in one of those nice middle-class families where education is encouraged and the family dynamics are non-toxic. I was stuck in Geraldton being raised by a brutal fundamentalist arsehole of a father until such a time as I could get out. That was the facts of the matter. No point pretending otherwise.

Mrs Lechski couldn't accept this though.

She was an old leftie, was Mrs Lechski; one of the old Whitlam-era Baby Boomers who are now pretty much extinct. She believed in education and society and all that horseshit. I didn't care about any of it. I didn't see what Whitlam or anyone else had ever done for me or why I should care.

Mrs Lechski was even a member of the local branch of the Australian Democrats. A truly thankless task in a town like Geraldton that had voted Wilson "Iron Bar" Tuckey in as our local member.

It was via this connection that she tried to help me again.

This was in the Keating era and there were scholarships back then promoted and funded by various left-wing groups designed to help bright kids from poor backgrounds into university. I think most of these things have folded since those days or at least I've not heard of them in years.

Mrs Lechski decided I should enter this one particular essay competition that was sponsored by some leftist journalist collective in Melbourne. The idea was to write an essay on the theme "The Australia I live in and the Australia I could live in". Basically you had to write about what was around you, good, bad and ugly and then paint a picture of how things could be better and give some sort of rough plan/idea for achieving that. I think the idea was to groom future leaders of the left. Like one day some kid who won the competition and went to university would become Prime Minister or whatever.

I had no real interest but Mrs Lechski insisted I write something for it.

I made a start but was struggling. What I found hard was trying to explain how to make things better. I had so little optimism at this point in my life that laying out a plan for reforming society into something fairer and better was just beyond me.

My father found out what I was doing and put his foot down.

'You think you're gonna go to the city and bludge around at university for four more years after you finish school? Always looking for the bludger's option, aren't you? You can forget about it, you're gonna get a job and earn a living like everyone else, boy.'

So the great attempt at getting myself a scholarship to university ended before it had even really begun.

I had to tell Mrs Lechski that I wasn't going to bother submitting an essay for the competition. I could see how disappointed she was. The one teacher I'd ever met who was worth a damn, the one teacher who actually gave a fuck and tried to help, and she was completely powerless to do anything.

The circumstances of my birth and who I'd been lumped with for parents meant that my life was an awful, soul-destroying struggle to get out from under, regardless of how bright a kid I may have been. Meanwhile, some utter deadhead mental mediocrity who lucked out and got born into a nice non-toxic middle-class family would sail through life without trying too hard. To me, the utter unfairness and cruelty of life has always been the most definitive proof of the non-existence of God. What all powerful and loving God could sit on his hands and allow this?

Something broke in my brain around this time. I went numb for several weeks, quiet, like a volcano just before it blows. It's probably lucky I had no access to firearms or I would have ended up a school shooter. As it was, I did the most spectacular act of vandalism in all my teenage years.

I had long been able to sneak out of the house without waking anyone up. I had a little backpack prepared with gloves, lighter, thick black Artline Texta, screwdriver, hammer and, of course, a Walkman and cassettes to provide the soundtrack to my epic vandalism spree. I snuck out sometime just before midnight and began.

First, I went to a patch of scrub a few streets over from the hospital. I wanted a diversion while I did other things so I did the tried-and-true method of diverting the attention of the local police. I started a fire. The scrub was tinder dry and full of rubbish; the fire was raging in a matter of minutes. I moved on quietly, unseen.

By the time I got to my high school I could hear the sirens and see the smoke looming over the night lights of our town.

I broke into the school without too much trouble. I got out my thick black Artline Texta and my Walkman. I chose the *In Utero* album as my soundtrack to vandalism and got to work. I don't remember choosing my slogan for that night's work. I don't recall a moment when it came to me what I would write. I just felt that it was what I wanted to say in that particular place and moment. With angry energy and with the strains of *Serve the Servants* in my ears, I wrote the same slogan over and over again all through the school.

WE KNOW WE HAVE NO FUTURE SO STOP LYING TO US

Of course, it was overly dramatic, but I was a maladjusted and abused 14-year-old, so what do you expect?

I wrote it all through the Science block, on desks and walls in big bold letters that would be impossible to ignore. I scrawled it across every surface I could find in the Maths block. I broke into the gym and emblazoned it through the change rooms.

Then I got to the English block.

I went into Mrs Lechski's class. I saw the desk she sat at. I remembered her attempts to encourage me and help me. I remembered how little difference it had made. I stood there for a moment thinking about how she'd tried and how it had actually made things worse not better.

Seized by a sudden rage I kicked off everything on her desk and scrawled my slogan in huge letters that couldn't be ignored. Then I opened the top drawer of the desk and pissed in it. My urine splashed all over whatever papers, pens and staplers were in that drawer.

Feeling a deep sense of satisfaction, I left the school and headed to the next target: my parents' church.

I'd actually vandalised it once before about six months earlier and never been caught but they had since installed a very basic alarm system. It was one of those old simple pad things you had to type in a code within forty seconds or else an ear-splitting alarm went off. Thing was, I had overheard one of the elders of the church talking when it had been installed. He was speaking to another elder and had casually mentioned that the code was 1951, the year he was born. It was apparently the only way he could remember it. At the time I filed it away in the back of my mind.

I broke the weak as piss lock with my screwdriver in a matter of seconds. Casually typed 1951 into the little pad and the alarm was deactivated, that simple.

I changed the tape in my Walkman, ejecting Nirvana and replacing it with the Black Album then got to work.

No fancy slogan was needed for my parent's church. Simply writing HAIL SATAN in huge letters on every available surface would be enough to send them into hysterics when they discovered it.

The night's work was done by the time the first side of the Black Album was played and I changed it over and headed for home.

News of my epic vandalism spree went around town very quickly. Nobody knew it was me, of course, and I enjoyed watching my parents and all the idiots in their church speculate. The favoured theory amongst them was that there was a secret satanic society hidden in town which was growing stronger because of all the immorality and wickedness in this awful, sinful society.

'It starts with rock music and young boys growing their hair long and before you know it abortion is legal, sodomy is celebrated and churches are vandalized like this,' one of the elders in the church declared. My parents and the rest of the faithful idiots nodded their heads in agreement.

School was different. The police were investigating and the headmaster told us all at assembly that he was certain they would soon find the culprit. I knew he was full of shit and smiled quietly to myself. Cops, like teachers, were morons. I knew this for a fact and was willing to risk punishment to prove it.

Mrs Lechski knew.

She never said anything but I knew she knew.

There was a hint of disappointment and defeat in her manner for the rest of the year. I quieted down a bit in her class. I felt slightly guilty but not enough to make me fess up to the crime. She made no further attempts to help me. I was just another student now. I think that's what hurt the most. She had reached out to try and help me. It had done no good. She didn't bother anymore.

Years passed. I never had her as a teacher again. I finished high school and as planned I fucked off to Perth as soon as I could. I tried to get a band started and make my mark as a musician but I had more enthusiasm than talent. Plus I got into drugs and wrote myself off for the first few years of my adulthood. It took years for me to get back on track and make something of my life.

I thought about her when I had my first book published. The memory of her trying to help the poor abused boy I had been back then touched me. I resolved to try and find her and let her know that she had made an impact. I wanted to let her know that I'd remembered her and she'd had a positive influence on my life.

But I couldn't find her. I googled her name and got nothing. Tried searching for her on various social media platforms and there was nothing. I even contacted my old school and asked them where she'd gone but the teachers working there now had never heard of her.

I wish I could find her and tell her I'm sorry. I wish I could let her know that she really did make a difference to me.

THE EVERLASTING

I remember the heat and the dust when I was young. The endless, merciless sunshine that baked the land and tanned your skin. I remember the grain trucks barrelling into town laden with wheat. I remember the trains and the dust from the silos.

I remember the local swimming pool in our town. I remember spending entire Saturdays there when I was a kid, so heavily saturated with chlorine that the smell of it stuck in our hair for days afterwards.

I remember fear. I remember fear, pain, guilt and humiliation. I remember growing up as a Jehovah's Witness in our little country town. Being marked off separate from the rest of the population because of our parents' religion. I remember the mind-numbing boredom of the Kingdom Hall on a Sunday. I remember listening to the utter bullshit the elders of our congregation spoke. I remember the despair at being forced to waste my youth on ancient Biblical nonsense.

I remember Beth, my friend, in truth the only friend I had when I was young. I remember her smile, I remember her hazel eyes with always a tinge of sadness to them, I remember her singing along to songs we knew and sounding pure, beautiful and true.

I remember her turning in on herself. I remember the years of darkness in the city as we both tried to stop the hurting.

I don't remember when I first met her or when we became friends. Merredin was not a big town and our little congregation of Jehovah's Witnesses was even smaller so we probably had known each other all our lives. I think we must have become friends when we both became teenagers and rebelled against the idiotic bullshit of our parents' religion.

If you had the good fortune not to be raised in a fundamentalist Christian cult then you may not really understand what it's like.

We were forced to be separate from the other kids at school because they were "worldly" and a bad influence. We were made to attend the Kingdom Hall and participate in the preaching activities in our congregation. We were fed constant fear and guilt and shame. Obedience was enforced with violence. The violence was condoned by their Bible. Many was the Sunday us kids sat in the Kingdom Hall uncomfortably because of hidden bruises while we wore our Sunday best and nodded like dumb sheep at the points the elders were making in their talk.

Kids growing up in fundamentalism learn to be sneaky. Beth and I snuck around and got away with as much forbidden fun as we could. We bonded in our rebellion and that bond would end up lasting a lifetime.

Inevitably as we progressed through high school the subject of escape became more and more pressing. Many years later I read a memoir of a British fighter pilot who was shot down and taken prisoner by the Germans during the war. He described how they'd get little snippets of news via Red Cross parcels and new prisoners being brought in and they'd realise the Allies were winning the war and gaining ground and that they'd soon be free again. He described how they heard that the Allies had landed at Normandy and began speculating how soon they'd be liberated. The hope kept them alive through the grim realities of life in a POW camp. It was much the same for us.

Beth was a year below me in high school. Each year of school we completed meant being one year closer to freedom. We talked about the day we would leave Merredin and our families.

'I don't care much what I do, I'll work at Macca's or whatever so long as I'm in the city and away from this bullshit.'

Beth and I were talking in my room. We'd been at the pool earlier in the day and now, having exhausted the entertainment possibilities of Merredin, we were hanging out in my room.

'Yeah, but fuck work and all that, I'm gonna get my band happening and get into the music scene in Perth. Find some cool people to start a band with and run with it,' I said as I strummed my acoustic guitar.

'How will you find people for your band?' Beth asked.

'I'll put a notice up at the record store. There's this one record store in Perth that has a notice board and people put up ads for starting a band all the time. Shitloads of bands have started up like that. There's all these new indie record labels, too, so once you're in the scene and you've got a band going it's easy to get signed.'

My youthful optimism was not challenged or questioned by Beth or myself at this time. Looking back now I just want to facepalm at my own teenage cluelessness.

I showed Beth the guitar tab books I'd bought during a recent trip to the city. I had the one for the Nirvana *Unplugged* album and I'd been learning it with a dedicated effort that I never put into school.

'Here I'll play and you sing,' I said, and started strumming the intro for *All Apologies*. Beth smiled shyly then started singing. It was beautiful.

All of a sudden she stopped! I knew he was at the door watching us before I even turned my head. But nonetheless I looked around.

There he was. The knuckle dragging fundamentalist thug who sired me. My father, my fucking arsehole father.

'You better not be playing that bloody satanic music in my house, boy,' he rumbled like a dumbed down thunder god.

'No Dad,' I said meekly as Beth and I kept our eyes down trying not to anger him.

He huffed, seemingly satisfied with this assertion of dominance, and headed out of the house for work.

Beth and I waited until he was gone before breathing easy again.

'Fuck, I hate him so much!' I practically spat the words. 'I'd love to cut his throat in his sleep.'

Beth sighed and nodded. 'How long is it now? Tell me again, I just need to hear it.'

We'd started counting the years, months, weeks and days until we could get out of there. It had started off as a bit of a joke but had become a coping mechanism. Like prisoners counting down the days until they were released.

'For me it's eleven months, three weeks and four days. For you, double that.'

She nodded, the gravity of those numbers weighing heavily on her mind.

The day did eventually come for me. I remember the phone calls organising a place to live with a cousin of mine who'd escaped a year earlier and was living in a share house in Maylands. Back in those days, before the mining boom and the greed of the housing investment craze, young people could rent out shitholes on the cheap and live on hardly any money for years at a time. My cousin Keith had shacked up with some other people his age in an old rundown red brick place in Maylands close to the Perth CBD. They'd had a housemate leave a few week before and I was right time and right place to take his room.

My arsehole father predicted my doom and refused to help in any way. I didn't care. I lugged my two bags and my guitar case to the Merredin train station myself; any price was worth paying for freedom.

Beth came to see me off. We stood together on the platform and talked of the future and she tried not to cry. I remember the crows were in the park next to the train station and were trying to raid one of the rubbish bins. They had managed to scatter some cans and wrappers but had found a dozen or so old chips and were feasting on the rewards of their efforts.

'You've got my address in Perth, haven't you? Keith says they still haven't got the phone on so you won't be able to ring me but we can write letters.'

'Yeah, I wrote it down and hid it. You won't forget about me, will you? I'm still stuck here for another whole year.'

'A year will pass quicker than you think, we'll get a place together when you come to the city, it'll be cool, just hold out until then.'

My train pulled in, we hugged, Beth lost the struggle against herself and cried a little bit. I got a bit of moisture in my eyes, too, if the truth be told but my overall feeling was one of liberation. The great day had come at last and I was getting out of Merredin and away from my stupid Bible thumping parents. I was free.

The train pulled out of Merredin. Beth stood on the platform and waved. I waved to her until I couldn't see her anymore. It was the last time I ever saw Merredin. I've never had the slightest interest in going back there in all the years since that moment.

I remember getting to East Perth Train Station some hours later. My cousin Keith was there to pick me up and take me to the place in Maylands.

It was a dump. The owners had obviously neglected it but the various young people who lived there hadn't helped the situation. The front lawn was waist-high weeds littered with a few empty goon bags and cans of VB. The cracked concrete driveway had more oil stains than clear concrete. There wasn't much furniture and what there was had a real "thrift shop" vibe to it. My room contained a mattress on the floor, an aluminium lasagne tray that was used as an ashtray and up on the wall a Metallica poster from the last time they toured Australia.

I loved it.

I settled in in no time. I got a job stacking shelves at the local Coles to pay the rent but I didn't really give a fuck about it. My focus was on getting my band together and getting into the Perth music scene. Jebediah were the local heroes at the time, they'd recently put out the *Slightly Odway* album and it was everywhere. Of course every scruffy white boy with a guitar thought they could do just as good, myself included.

I was writing a letter a week to Beth at this time and getting back the same. I'd tell her about the gigs I was going to, the new up and coming bands I was seeing and the connections I was making in the scene. I remember one letter I wrote telling her that I had a bass player and a rhythm guitarist lined up and all I needed was a drummer and a singer and my band would be ready to conquer the world.

It was, of course, mostly fantasy.

In reality I was terminally shy and a totally clueless bumpkin with no idea how to move amongst cool music people in the city. I'd go to gigs and stand in the corner, nursing a beer and watching the bands, wishing I could be the one on stage.

What really doomed my musical ambitions however was the drugs. I'd dived headfirst into drugs and drink since arriving in the city. Our sharehouse, like a lot of sharehouses in the 90s, had a bucket bong permanently set up in the loungeroom. Alcohol was a lot cheaper back then, the taxes weren't so high; so getting properly pissed was a cheap hobby that we indulged in a lot.

And then I discovered heroin.

Perth was awash with heroin in the late 90s. So were most Australian cities but Perth was worse because of our port and the trade routes from South East Asia. The poppy fields of Cambodia and Afghanistan were working overtime in those days.

What little I knew about it beforehand came from books about musicians. I knew that most of the best music in the last 50 years had been made by heroin addicts: Keith Richards, Lou Reed, David Bowie, Iggy Pop, Kurt Cobain. It's an impressive list and probably the best advertisement for the stuff.

I first saw it from a friend of one of the guys in our sharehouse. He was doing it casually at the chipped wreck of a kitchen table we had. I was about twelve Ouzo and Cokes deep into the night at this point so all I did was watch, fascinated by the whole process. It was thrilling to me, transgressive and forbidden. If there is one thing kids who grow up in Fundamentalist Christianity learn it's that fun things are forbidden and the more forbidden and shocking something is, the more fun it is likely to be. Thus the whole sleazy, dark and forbidden vibe of heroin is what made it attractive to me. *My parents, their religion and society hate this? Must be awesome!* was how my brain worked.

A few weeks later I tried it for the first time. A girl named Kim who was also stacking shelves at Coles had become friendly with me. I'd been to her place for parties once or twice and got properly wasted along with everyone else.

One night we both knocked off at the same time. We were walking in roughly the same direction and she asked me if I wanted to come around.

Once we got there I got a weird vibe. She was sharing the place with about four other people which was fairly normal but two of them, a couple, were older than us by about ten years. This was odd as sharehousing was a young person's game, or so I thought. The older couple were named Valerie and Carl. In about five minutes I discovered that they were regular heroin users, hence why they were still living the impoverished sharehouse lifestyle well into their 30s. In another five minutes I discovered that Kim had recently started using heroin as well.

Kim had brought me along as a kind of "designated driver" or a person not on heroin who could supervise the heroin users and make sure they didn't die on the couch. Apparently they'd had a close call the week before and were a bit nervous about it.

I sat there smoking and watching them go through their elaborate ritual. I was mesmerised by it all. Is this what all those musicians did? I thought, is this what happened backstage at so many classic gigs? Is this what inspired Lou Reed and Kurt Cobain?

I made myself a cup of tea and sat and watched them as they nodded off and enjoyed their quiet personal bliss that an uninitiated person couldn't begin to comprehend.

I made my decision.

When Valerie emerged from a deep nod into a short period of relative lucidity I hit her up for a taste.

'I want to try it,' I said, 'just a little bit though, I've never done it before. I've probably got no tolerance.'

'Sure,' she slurred, one eye still closed in sweet opiate numbness while she sorted out a clean needle and a tourniquet for me. The amount she gave me would have been barely a sniff for an experienced user but it was enough to send me away to a fluffy brown Cambodian cloud where pain and hurt did not exist and life was but a dream.

I was off and running.

Life went downhill fairly quickly after that. The beer and bongs lifestyle I had been living was fairly sustainable. I was able to hold down my job at Coles and pay rent while indulging. This was not the case with heroin. The job at Coles went, Kim also left about the same time. I never saw her again and I don't know what happened to her; nothing good is a safe bet. I got kicked out of the sharehouse for not paying rent and leaving needles around the place. I went through a quick succession of addresses in the next few months. I lost contact with Beth about this time, writing letters wasn't something I was capable of while trying to maintain a small but growing heroin habit.

Things got ugly and continued to get uglier. Looking back I was only using for just over a year, maybe a year and a half, but that was enough. I good and properly fucked myself.

The darkness I was living in was apparent to me and I began to try and look for a way out. In the end it was Beth who saved me.

There was a dealer at this time by the name of Hami. I don't know if that was his real name or a nickname but he was well known to everyone in the drug scene in Perth in those days. He looked like a lanky, wog version of Elvis, or rather like a stick thin junkie trying to be an Elvis impersonator. He lived in these flats in Victoria Park which were known drug and crime hotspots. This was twenty odd years ago; Victoria Park has been cleaned up and colonised by Hipsters now. Where the smack deals used to happen there are now craft beers and Thai food.

The ritual which everyone had to perform was to knock on Hami's door and take three steps back. He'd be watching you through a peephole and if you didn't do it, if you fucked around at all, no drugs for you.

I knocked on his door this day and took the obligatory three steps back when around the corner came Beth. I knew as soon as I looked at her that she was using as well.

There should be some sort of modern etiquette guide that tells you how to deal with seeing someone you went to school with buying drugs from the same dealer as you. Like what do you do? Pretend you don't see them? Say nothing and feel awkward? Or maybe you should roll with it and be friendly? Be all like "Oh hi, haven't seen you in years, so you do smack now, too?"

Hami invited us in, asked us how much we wanted, took our money and went to another room to get it sorted. The ritual of scoring from Hami was that he went to the other room and you sat there quietly on the couch and did not move or speak. This was enforced by his missus, a fat sweaty blob of a woman whom we called "Jabba the slut" behind her back. She would sit there watching videos, always watching videos no matter what time of the day you went there. She must have spent a fortune at Video Ezy. If you made a noise or moved from the couch she'd bark at you. If she barked loud enough Hami would come back and depending on how upset she was, you'd either get no drugs or possibly a beating if the offence was grave enough.

Beth and I sat there this day, wanting to talk, wanting to re-establish the connection we'd once had but not daring to because we feared being cut off from our drugs. Hami's missus sat there glued to the screen watching some god-awful Jean-Claude Van Damme movie, her blank face completely absorbed in the idiotic excuse for a plot. Tentatively, with my heart on a string, I reached out for Beth's hand. I touched it and gave her a brief, tender squeeze. She squeezed back. There was hope and the tiniest sliver of happiness for the first time in a long time.

Hami came out and gave us our drugs and we left.

Once outside the door we could talk freely. The questions came tumbling out faster than we could answer them. How had we both ended up here? Where were you living now? That sort of thing. Of course because we'd both just scored the obvious question was did we have some place to go and fix?

'I was going to use the toilets at the Vic Park Library, they're always clean and quiet and I usually just hang out at the library afterwards, nobody bothers you much,' Beth said.

'I'm living just down the train line at Queens Park, you can come to my place if you want.' She accepted and we headed to the train station.

The place I was living in was an utter dive. It was a granny flat out the back of an old Greek lady's house. I was paying peanuts for the rent and she insisted I pay in cash; I'm pretty sure she never told the tax man about it. I had no furniture other than a mattress on the floor. My only possessions at this time were a bag of clothes, mostly filthy and rarely washed; a kettle I had actually stolen from Kmart, and an old radio that I had tried to hock at Cash Converters but they'd said it wasn't worth anything. My diet at this time was two-minute noodles and iced coffees and cigarettes. I have never been that thin before or since.

We got down to business, mixing and fixing with admirable efficiency, once happily sedated, we began, tentatively and with a certain delicate caution, to talk about our lives.

Beth had come down to the city almost exactly a year after I'd left. I'd already got on this dismal merry-go-round of addiction by then so I'd lost contact with her. She thought it would be easy to find me again in Perth and got a room in the YWCA in East Perth until she found something more permanent. At some point she'd fallen into the same trap as me and here we were.

I listened sympathetically but something about it bothered me. There was something she wasn't telling me. Something not mentioned, something out of sight and off limits. I didn't push or ask difficult questions but I was aware it was there.

Without it ever being formally discussed Beth moved in with me after that day and we became inseparable again. A sort of twisted, derelict and despairing version of the friendship we'd had in high school. On the one hand it was good to have a friend again, someone to share those quiet moments with and pooling our meagre finances also helped a lot. On the other hand, I couldn't help but be horrified by what we'd become in such a short period of time. All through those miserable years in Merredin we'd had hope; it was only the hope of escape but it was nonetheless hope. Now we had nothing. We were junkies. We wandered through the streets of Perth like cockroaches, invisible and ignored by the normal people except as pests to be removed.

How has this happened? How did we both fuck up so badly?

I had no answers at the time, I was too focused on surviving. Now though, with the benefit of twenty years or so clean, I can look at it with a clearer head.

Basically, the way I see it now is that the Jehovah's Witness cult we'd been raised in had traumatised us to the point where we were unable to function and cope in the normal world. Add in the cult had kept us out of the normal world and we hadn't developed the normal skills to cope with life. Add in stupidity on our part and you have an almost perfect recipe for kids like us to fuck up their lives before they've even really begun to live.

I suspect there must be thousands of kids like Beth and I out there. Raised in that idiotic cult, so desperate to escape they launch themselves unprepared into the merciless world. Their failure is pre-ordained. I'd be surprised if a certain percentage of them don't go back to the cult with their tails between their legs, defeated by the real world and desperate for stability, even the stability of captivity.

For about three or four months, Beth lived with me in that little granny flat in Queens Park. We took the train into the city to get our drugs, scam some money and do what we needed to do. We slept on my grotty mattress and listened to my old radio in the evenings. Beth showed me the Hare Krishna place in Northbridge where you could get a feed for two dollars. I taught Beth some scams that I'd learnt and we managed to make our money stretch far enough that we didn't get sick very often.

I began to think about finding a way out of this life. I discovered there was a detox facility just near McIver station. I went in and spoke to a drug counsellor. He told me about my "options for treatment" and I thought long and hard about it. I talked to Beth one night as we lay on the mattress and listened to the news on the radio.

'So he reckons I can get into the detox, do the week or so it takes and then go to this Serenity Lodge place down in Rockingham. That's a three month rehab thing. I'm thinking it's a good idea, this can't go on forever. What do you think?'

Beth absorbed this information with an exhausted expression on her face. That's the thing they don't show in the movies, how exhausting it is being a junkie, how it grinds you down and saps your will to live. It really isn't sustainable.

'Sounds alright, I'm keen if you are, and you're right, this can't go on.'

It had been spoken. A decision had been made. The wheels moved surprisingly quickly from that point onwards.

I went in first. Beth came into the detox four days after me. By that point I was well and truly suffering and I was overjoyed to see a friendly face. Beth went through her own withdrawal hell and joined me in Serenity Lodge a week or so later.

The whole rehab experience was a little bit tedious to be honest. Classes, therapy sessions, talking to counsellors and getting bussed to NA meetings in the evenings; not my idea of a fun time but it wasn't too bad. More importantly we were clean and we had the feeling that we were making progress. Things were getting tangibly better. We were both malnourished, having lived on the worst possible diet for a year or so. The food in the rehab wasn't great but it was real food and fattened us up a bit.

The other people in the rehab didn't interest me much. Fellow fuck ups who decided to try walking the straight and narrow with varying degrees of enthusiasm. Good for them but I didn't care; I was out to pull my life out of the gutter and bring Beth with me. If they all relapsed and died tomorrow it wouldn't change anything.

I finished the program first and left the rehab feeling better than I had in years. I rented a little place in Wanneroo and waited for Beth to join me. I made a decision that I was sick of being on the dole so I took the first job I could get, stacking shelves at Woolworths. I had made no progress apparently but I didn't let it bother me. I had money coming in; I was clean and healthier than I'd been in years. I was reunited with Beth who was also clean now; it felt like the future was brighter than it had ever been.

It lasted eleven months.

Beth and I were in a happy little routine for a while. I look back on it now as a golden age. I had a job, she was still on the dole, we lived in my little flat like the best of housemates. I used the money from my job to be a little domestic and house-proud for the first time in my life. I bought furniture from a real furniture shop for the first time ever. It was a deeply satisfying experience.

I got a second hand car cheap and that expanded our options a lot. We made a habit of going to the beach nearly every day. We hardly ever swam, our bodies still bore the marks of our addiction and we were horribly self-conscious about it, but we'd often get some fish and chips and just watch the waves for hours. It still stands out in my mind as one of the happiest times of my life.

Beth and I had attended NA meetings while in rehab and for a while afterwards. I wasn't that keen on it all. I didn't, and still don't, believe that our problems were because of a drug. We needed to get over being raised as Jehovah's Witnesses, that was the recovery we needed. Everything else stemmed from that.

Beth kind of took to it. I think she liked the feeling of not being in this mess all alone. Having others who'd suffered and who were struggling to get up and out at the same time, it was a comfort to her.

So I attended the meetings sporadically but Beth was a regular. She made friends with the people there and they seemed to have a positive influence on her. Sometimes on my days off work we'd go together and then hang out afterwards. I didn't mind the people from the meetings, they were mostly alright, just battlers trying to get their lives back together. It was just that I didn't care that much about them. My world was Beth and myself. I struggled to connect on any deep level with anything else.

Beth met Andy at the main lunchtime NA meeting in the city. I didn't like him from the moment I saw him. A skinny red head with white boy dreads and a Korn t-shirt, may as well put up a sign saying "I'm a fuckwit" with a look like that.

She began spending more and more time with him. Going for coffee after the meetings and things like that. I didn't approve but in the end I was her friend and not her father. But I felt like I was losing her.

My suspicions were confirmed soon enough. She started staying overnight at Andy's place. I really didn't approve but what could I do? To me it was obvious the guy was a fuckwit and would lead her nowhere good but you try telling a young woman anything.

Inevitably the day came when she left me. I remember it well, like a rupture in time, a still tender bruise on the story of my life.

I came back home from a shift at Woollies exhausted and thinking only of food and bed. She was waiting up for me.

'Luke, I have some news.'

I knew what she was going to say.

'Andy and I are going to go to Melbourne. He has family and friends over there, we're going to start a new life together. Andy has contacts in the film industry and the music scene over there, he can make good money directing music videos for all the new bands coming out of the Melbourne scene. It's a big opportunity for both of us.'

74

I knew it was all bullshit. Andy was a moron and a degenerate. I was willing to put down money that he would go back to using drugs and drag Beth down with him. It was all so obvious.

But of course I couldn't convince Beth of that.

I dumbly agreed and pretended to wish them both the best. Then she gave me the coup de grace.

'We're flying out in two days. Could you give us a lift to the airport?'

Like a meek cuckolded husband, I agreed.

The day came. I gave them a lift to the airport. Beth hugged me goodbye and Andy talked bullshit about all the things he was going to do in Melbourne. They left. I stayed. I went back to my flat in Wanneroo and watched TV for a couple of hours then drove down to the beach to watch the sunset and feel sorry for myself.

Beth kept in touch for a few months. I got semi-regular letters and once or twice a postcard but I didn't believe for a second that wonderful things were happening for her and Andy in Melbourne. Pretty soon the letters stopped.

My life in Perth was quiet. I had stopped bothering with the NA meetings when Beth left. I didn't have a single friend in the whole city. I went to the local library on Sunday afternoons and got myself something to read for the week. I still got fish and chips and sat on the beach in the evenings. I sometimes went days without talking to anyone. The city is a lonely place when you have nobody.

In the end I decided to get out. I didn't have a plan, I knew I was never going back to Merredin, I knew I didn't want to live in the city anymore and I had a strong desire to be next to the sea all the rest of my life. So I travelled from beach town to beach town. I worked whatever casual job I could find; bottle shops, pubs, servos and local supermarkets, it didn't matter to me. I was numb.

I drifted, going wherever I felt drawn at the time, working at whatever job was available and leaving again when it suited me. I went as far north as Broome and as far south as Esperance. The longest I stayed in one place was two years. Mostly I stayed about a year. I did a stint at nearly every beach town in Western Australia. Jurien Bay, Denham, Augusta, Albany and Margaret River, I did them all. Nobody bothered me or criticised my lifestyle. I think the locals understood the impulse to drift through life and since I worked rather than collecting the dole and I didn't cause any trouble or bother anyone they were inclined to leave me be.

All up it lasted twelve years.

Twelve years of total aimlessness. Twelve years of sitting on beaches in the evenings looking at the horizon thinking those big looking at the horizon thoughts.

Eventually it takes a toll on you.

I settled down in Busselton. The mining boom was still on and everyone was chasing big money in the mines up north. I had no interest in big money but I felt the need to settle. The local council was having trouble getting workers. I came along at just the right time.

I got a job driving the sweeper truck. It was steady and regular. I began to socialise, tentatively at first, with some of the blokes from work. I met a woman, local girl; we became an item; after a year together she had an "accident" and got pregnant. We got married and settled into family life.

I still sometimes went to the beach in the evenings, looked at the horizon and thought those big looking at the horizon thoughts but it was less of a regular thing now. I had a wife and a daughter and that seemed to give me enough reason to live.

I got a letter from my mother when my daughter was about a year old. Fatherhood had given me a great deal of happiness to the point where I'd mostly stopped thinking about all those miserable years growing up in Merredin. I hadn't had any contact with my family from the time I'd caught the train to Perth all those years ago. They were strangers to me and I was slightly baffled to see the letter from my mother. How had she found my address? Why was she contacting me?

I opened it and read.

Dear Luke,
I know you have rejected your family and Jehovah's Kingdom but I have spent weeks trying to find where you lived now so I could give you some important news. Your father has cancer and is dying. It is very sad and only our faith in Jehovah and His Kingdom is keeping our spirits up in this trying time.

Now might be a good time for you to repent and come see your father one last time in this wicked world. He has the hope of seeing us again in Jehovah's Kingdom but with the sinful life you've no doubt led we can't be sure of seeing you there. Repent now and seek forgiveness from Jehovah and your father.

Your loving mother,
Janet.

I had to read it several times to make sure it said what it said. I had been out of the cult for so long the toxicity of it was almost alien to me now but as I read my mother's letter it all came flooding back.

The old hate stirred in me. For a moment I thought about crafting an eloquent reply expressing how much I hated my father and despised my mother. But then I wondered what that would achieve. Nothing. The stupid bitch would take it as proof of my sin and wickedness and feel vindicated.

In the end, after half an hour of thinking about it, I put the letter in the bin and never replied to it. I never received another one and I never told my wife about it. My youth was dead and buried. As if it had never happened.

My wife and I had another daughter. I stayed in my council job and was more or less content with my life. A few more years went by. I saw my first grey hair in the mirror one morning and realised how old I was getting. My wife and I had a third daughter. I marked ten years of working for the council by using a week's leave to stay home and sleep in.

My wife and daughters filled whatever hole inside me that growing up in a cult had created. They healed whatever scars had been caused by those hard and bitter times in the city when I was young. Until you've had a little girl hold your hand and call you "Daddy" you don't really understand how much it means. I was happy with my life, something I would never have predicted when I was younger.

I hadn't got into the whole social media thing. There was nobody I really wanted to keep contact with. I didn't see the point of having people I'd been in high school with able to see what I was doing now. The people I'd known when I was doing drugs, well, I assumed they'd all be dead by now, and as for the years I was drifting from one small beach town to another, I'd made no serious connections in that time and I would struggle to remember the names of the people I'd met. I was a man without a past. Or rather I had a past but it was dead to me and I didn't speak about it. Even my wife didn't know the full story. I'd vaguely told her that I'd had a "rough time growing up" and drifted around for a few years but I never went into more details than that.

My wife was on social media, however. I don't know why, half the people she'd gone to high school with had never left

Busselton and she saw them down the street every week. She could have just talked to them in person rather than via a computer.

Anyway, my wife had taken my surname, old fashioned maybe but that's how it was. One day out of the blue she got a message asking if she was related to me and knew where I was.

The message was from Beth.

She showed it me and it all came back to me. The loss and hopelessness of those years. The friendship that had held us together and got us out of the dark pit of addiction. It was like being hit by a truck you thought was safely past and gone.

My wife asked me who Beth was. I still wasn't comfortable telling everything. I thought for a few seconds and decided on the option that didn't tell everything but also didn't lie.

'She was my friend, we grew up together, lived in the city together for a few years but she went to Melbourne. I thought she was dead. I'm glad to hear she's not.'

'So you want to talk to her?'

'Yeah I suppose so. I don't know what she's been up to all these years. Can you reply to her message and give her the postal address? Tell her I'm not on social media and I'm a bit of a Luddite so it's going to have to be old fashioned letters.'

My wife relayed my message and Beth replied within minutes.

'Of course he's not up with the times, he probably still listens to 90s music only, doesn't he? Ha ha, tell him I'll get to writing a letter right away and send it as soon as it's done.'

My wife was much amused by Beth's correct guess about my music tastes and attitude to the modern world. 'She knows you well,' she laughed.

A bit over a week later I got a letter from Beth. I held it in my hand like some sacred relic for a few moments. I looked at the return address on the back. It was a PO Box in the suburbs of Canberra. What the fuck was she doing living in Canberra of all places?

I opened it and began to read.

Dear Luke,

I am so glad to find you alive and apparently happy after so many years. I never forgot you and never stopped hoping you were alright. I see you are a husband and father now. It suits you.

I have a daughter myself, her name is Emma and she is 19. Her father is Andy, yes that Andy, let me just say you were right about him. Things went to shit almost as soon as we got to Melbourne. We both started using again and there were some ugly times. It took two trips to rehab for me to get clean for good. Andy never got his shit together and died of an overdose when Emma was two.

Being a single mum and trying to stay clean was not easy but I managed.

I met someone else, someone who was actually a force for good in my life, her name is Kate, she is a Doctor and we have been together nearly fifteen years now. We got married as soon as it became legal and have a very happy home together.

Kate works at a hospital here in Canberra. I went back to school and got an English degree at the University of Canberra a few years back. Emma has grown up in a happy home full of love, we have supported and encouraged her in her education and she is now studying medicine at ANU. She wants to be a doctor like Kate.

I have to tell you something, it is one of those big life things that are never easy to tell so I can't see any way forward other than just getting it out.

Do you remember the year I was left behind in Merredin after you went to Perth? Do you remember one of the elders in our congregation by the name of Rodney Hetfield? We all called him "Brother Rod" or "Elder Rod" as I recall.

Well, and there is no easy way to tell this story, after you left he must have decided I was easy pickings, unprotected lamb or something like that. He started coming around our house more and more, eventually he got me alone and raped me.

It was years before I could talk about this. Kate has helped me immensely, she hooked me up with a good therapist and I have worked through a lot of this stuff.

Anyway, and here is the reason for my reaching out after so many years. In our beloved home state of Western Australia (that's sarcasm but maybe you love the place, I don't know) they have recently amended the law regarding sexual abuse of children. There is now no statue of limitations. Meaning that I can move forward with a prosecution of "Elder Rod" if I want.

I have contacted the sex crimes branch of the WA Police and made a statement. The nice lady detective I spoke to told me I'm not the only person who has made complaints about this individual and if I wanted to proceed they are cautiously optimistic they can get a conviction. After discussing it with Kate and Emma I have decided to proceed.

So I am coming to Perth in a month's time. It would mean a lot to me if I could have the support of my oldest friend in what is sure to be an unpleasant time. Write me back and let's make arrangements to meet up in the city where we spent our youth in darkness so that we can spend our middle age in light.

Your friend always,
Beth

I had to sit quietly and think about that letter for some time.

There is no moment when a man feels more useless than when a woman he cares about tells him she was raped years ago. You are utterly redundant and helpless at that point. The event was years ago, you can't protect her or avenge her and you are a useless, if sympathetic, lump.

I thought for a long time about all that Beth and I had lost over the years. How much the cult our parents had raised us in had cost us. What made it even more unfair and enraging was that neither Beth nor myself had ever voluntarily participated in the Jehovah's Witness cult ourselves. We had been forced to under threat of violence from our parents. Yet it had marred our lives so thoroughly that even now, when we were in our 40s, we still suffered from it.

Where was the justice in that? By what right did our idiot parents inflict a lifetime of misery on us because they were gullible enough to believe in this nonsense? How many other kids had this happened to? How many lives were marred beyond hope of redemption by this awful cult?

After I settled down and let the anger subside I wrote back to Beth and told her I'd love to see her again. I gave my phone number and some suggestions for meeting up in Perth.

The day we met in Perth was glorious. As though the Gods had decided that we deserved only the best weather.

We had arranged to meet at Perth Zoo. I'd brought the wife and kids up for the weekend and we thought we may as well make a trip out of it. We met Beth outside the front gate. She was standing there with Kate and Emma. She looked older, obviously, there was a slight suggestion of life having battered her around in her appearance but otherwise she looked healthy and happy enough.

Kate seemed a nice person if a little on the posh side. Emma looked a bit like Andy, same red hair and skinny build, but she seemed like a nice kid, a lot more switched on than either Beth or myself was at that age. I introduced my wife and daughters to Beth and her family. Beth fussed over my girls a lot; she thought they were adorable and said so loudly and often.

It was a real sweet moment, standing outside the front gate of the Perth Zoo. For a few minutes it felt like the past was healed and everything had worked out alright after all. Just for a moment.

We went and pottered around the various exhibits for a while. My wife hit it off with Kate and Emma which made me happy. Beth hung near me and doted on my girls when they came close to her.

Eventually, Beth and I separated from the others and sat down at a table to talk. The Zoo continued being the Zoo around us while we discussed the wreckage of our youth and what we'd been able to salvage out of our lives.

Beth told me about the ugly times in Melbourne with Andy, the struggle to get clean again and raise Emma on her own. She told me about meeting Kate at a university women's group and discovering that there was a spark there. She told me about settling down and building a life, her own slice of happily ever after, with Kate and Emma in Canberra. She told me about watching Emma grow up and be happy, so unlike her own youth that she found it almost unreal.

A school group went past where we were sitting, noisy and excited kids making conversation impossible for a few minutes.

It was my turn to speak.

I told Beth about after she'd left and how alone and lonely I'd been in Perth. I told her about my years of drifting, living in one beach town after another. Going everywhere but belonging nowhere. A loner without roots, a traveller without a destination. I told her about settling down in Busselton, meeting my wife and having my daughters. I told her about the happiness my girls had given me, about what it meant to have a little person call you Dad and hold your hand. I told her about the simple pleasures of being a husband and father and the meaning it had given my life.

We sat and digested each other's story for a few minutes. Families and kids walked past and the Zoo was just beautiful in the sunshine.

'It almost seems like we've both managed to turn out alright in the end, doesn't it?' she said.

'It does,' I conceded.

'And yet there are things that haven't healed, aren't there?'

'There are.'

She began to tell me about the case she was here to be a part of. There were several other victims of "Brother Rod" who had come forth. Apparently he had made a habit of preying on teenage girls in the congregation and the Jehovah's Witness organization had shuffled him around the state to try and keep scandals from brewing. This is what made the WA Police Sex Crimes Branch so eager to prosecute. It seems the Jehovah's Witness hierarchy had a habit of doing this and ignoring complaints from victims. The Police wanted a conviction and a scalp to try and highlight their misdeeds and encourage more victims to come forth. They also wanted to prosecute some of the hierarchy for non-reporting of crimes against children. They hoped that a conviction or two might be a shot across the bows of the JW cult and might lead to reform.

'I think they're being optimistic as far as that goes,' I said. 'Those bastards will never admit they did anything wrong. They won't change and won't reform but a few convictions might alert the public to how they really are.'

Beth thought it over for a minute.

'I'm not so sure. If they get a couple of convictions that might open the door to civil suits. If the Jehovah's Witness organization loses court cases and has to pay up big time to victims, they might adjust their way of doing things. Not because they want to but because it gets too expensive not to.'

I thought about it.

'So is that why you're doing this? To prevent other kids in the future suffering? Or is it just a sense of justice and making sure the right thing gets done? Or is it just plain revenge?'

She looked away for a moment before cautiously speaking, her voice subdued and fragile in contrast to the noisy children racing around the Zoo.

'Have you ever been in touch with your parents after you left?'

'No, Mum sent me a letter a few years ago, I don't know how she got my address. She told me my Dad was dying of cancer and that I should come crawling back for his forgiveness before he died. I put it in the bin and never replied. I assume Dad must have died shortly after but I don't care. They aren't people, they're cult zombies, and you can't have a relationship with cult zombies. I accepted the idea that I was essentially an orphan a long time ago. It's unfortunate, it's unlucky. All the parents in the world and I got lumped with cult zombies, but that's life.'

I shrugged. I'd accepted this fact a long time ago but voicing it out loud was still unpleasant. I waited for Beth to respond.

'I rang my Mum just before Emma was born. Well, maybe like three months before. Anyway, I wanted to tell her about her new grandchild; I still thought there might be a normal human being under the cult zombie. I was wrong.'

'She screamed at me, called me a slut and disappointment for a daughter. Said I deserved to die in childbirth for my sin.

Slammed down the phone on me. I was hanging by a string at the time, I'd got clean once I found out I was pregnant but I was still broke and struggling and looking down the barrel of being a single mum on welfare. I think the only thing that kept me from chucking it all in was my baby. I was determined that Emma was going to have a better life than mine.'

'Then about two years ago I had a cancer scare. In my lungs, they got it in time but it was a scary moment. Having a death sentence, or what you think is a death sentence, really focuses the mind, makes you think about what really matters in life. I did the whole "looking over my life so far" thing, I think maybe everyone who has cancer does that on some level, and I was appalled to realise how much of my life had been spent either directly suffering under the cult or dealing with after-effects. Being with Kate, seeing her family and how healthy and functional they are, really made me think about my family and how fucked they are.'

'Have you ever thought about how unlucky we are, Luke? Of all the potential parents in the world, we got lumped with white trash cult zombies. Kate works with a lovely Sudanese doctor who was born in a refugee camp. It was easier for him to make something of his life here than it has been for us to overcome growing up in the Jehovah's Witness cult. Stop and think about that.'

'After the cancer scare, I thought about how much time I might have left. Technically I'm still "in remission" so it could come back and the likelihood of surviving it twice is lower. How much of my life have I already lived? How much of it has been marred and ruined by a cult I never chose to join? How long do I have left and what am I going to spend my time doing?'

'I decided they have to pay for what they took from me. Not just the rape and the years of dealing with that trauma but also just the sheer amount of time in my life that I will never get back. There has to be some sort of justice, or reckoning or payback, whatever you want to call it, for what they took from me.'

She stopped there, exhausted from laying it all out. She shrugged as if to say "that's my lot" and looked out over the lawn where school kids were running wild beyond the control of their teachers and parents.

I didn't know what to say so I remained silent. I had my sunnies on and I looked up at the blue and cloud-sprinkled Western Australian sky as I thought about what she'd said. I thought about when she'd lived with me in that dump in Queens Park, less than ten Ks from the Zoo now I thought about it. I thought about how we'd caught the train into the city most days to grind our miserable way through another day of the junkie life. I thought of all the time that had passed since that time. I imagined someone up in this beautiful blue sky, a God or an Angel perhaps, watching and observing the lives we'd lived, a compassionate witness to the pity of our years.

My attention was drawn back to Earth by Beth's hand. She'd reached out across the table and squeezed my hand the exact same way I'd once squeezed hers that day at Hami's when we'd found each other again. I squeezed back. We were friends for life.

Things moved fast after that. The trial began. I used up my leave from work to attend, sitting in the court in Perth and watching the proceedings. The media took an interest, religious sleaze bags always made good headlines. I sat next to a reporter from Channel 9 the first day who scribbled notes the whole time.

"Brother Rod" looked like shit. Time hadn't been kind to him. He looked like a sad old man confused by the world around him. He saw me in the public gallery and I'm pretty sure he recognised me. The cold look of hate he flashed me convinced me he remembered me and knew why I was there. Mostly he just looked forward and his lawyer did all the talking.

Beth and the other victims spoke via video link from some sort of women's refuge place. A couple of the women had a counsellor person sitting next to them as they spoke. Their testimony was coherent, plain and truthful. The details were all similar, which seemed fairly damning to me. The defence lawyer tried to trip them up but they all stuck to their story and held their own.

In the end the jury was convinced. Guilty on four counts of rape of a minor, guilty on a couple of lesser charges as well. I watched Rod's face as the jury gave their verdict. I was hoping he would crack and breakdown and cry but he maintained a stoic expression on his face the entire time.

Because the jury had taken such a short time to reach a verdict we had a free day in the city. Beth and I wandered over to Northbridge for lunch. We found a Chinese place and got a table next to the window where we could observe the passing parade.

We ate quietly and stared out the window for long periods of time. We felt no need to discuss the trial now that it was over.

'James Street hasn't changed that much in 20-odd years has it?' Beth spoke as a couple of junkies walked past the window.

'No, some things never change,' I said as I watched them go. 'How long is it exactly? Twenty-three years, I think? Twenty-three years ago we were like those two. Fucking hopeless. Now here we are.'

'Maybe those two will be smart enough or lucky enough to end up like us. Maybe in twenty-three years time they'll be looking back on their wasted youth like we are. Life goes on, for those who don't die it goes on. The dead, of course, get forgotten. Remember Hami? I wonder what happened to him? Remember that guy, the one with the bung eye that we used to score off, what was his name? Where are any of those people now? Unclaimed bodies in the morgues of public hospitals probably, used by medical students to learn anatomy and then cremated. Dust and ashes, nobody but us even remembers them and when we die they will be fully forgotten, as though they never existed.'

'How did those people end up in the drug life in the first place?' I continued. 'Were they traumatised kids like we were? Damaged from fucked up families? There's a good chance they were. When you think about it like that, it seems very unfair. A child is born with whatever potential and because they have fucked up parents they become damaged goods and end up a junkie. Then the junkie life kills them and they are forgotten, unremembered and unloved. Meanwhile some total dipshit of a kid lucks out and gets born into a nice, functional middle class family so he gets to live a nice happy life and dies at a ripe old age surrounded by a loving family. You will never convince me a just and loving God exists, not with the complete unfairness of life.'

I finished my rant and looked out the window, absorbed in my own thoughts. I felt Beth's hand reach out for me again. She gave my hand a squeeze, just like I'd squeezed her hand all those years ago at Hami's place. I squeezed back. For a moment it was alright, we had beaten the odds. Beth had got justice, we'd survived.

We were the lucky ones.

I had to go back to Busselton shortly after so I didn't stay around for the sentencing. Rod got a decent whack of time in prison, given his age and health it meant he would almost certainly die in prison. Justice had been done for a change.

There was a bit of media coverage of the trial and Beth and one of the other women spoke to the media about it. The Jehovah's Witness organization predictably circled the wagons and refused to comment. The general public were alerted to what kind of toxic cult they were and hopefully some people were dissuaded from joining their ranks; maybe a few decent people even left, it was probably the best that could be hoped for.

Beth and her little family went back to Canberra to continue their lives. I stayed in Busselton with my family and continued mine. Beth and I wrote to each other regularly for almost a year after the trial. I enjoyed our little correspondence immensely.

My wife and my daughters were happy and healthy. We had a happy and loving family. I had my little slice of happily ever after.

About a year after the trial Beth wrote to me that her cancer had returned. It wasn't looking good. The doctors didn't like the look of it and were advising her to prepare for the worst. She had Kate and Emma looking after her as best they could. She kept writing every other week but the situation got worse. In the end she told me point blank that this would be her last letter and if I wanted to see her one last time it was now or never.

I had never been to Canberra before. I got a motel room and a hire car and managed to navigate my way around the place without too much drama. It was freezing cold and miserable; I'd come at the wrong time of year.

Beth looked like a skeleton. It was frightening. The cancer had run through her quicker than anybody could have foreseen. She was nearly at the end and there was no point bullshitting about it.

I sat down carefully in the plastic chair next to her bed. Various tubes travelled in and out of Beth, various machines beeped and whirred around her; it was awful. Her eyes were closed but she didn't seem asleep. I gently squeezed her hand, she squeezed back and a smile crossed her face.

'Luke, you made it!'

'Of course I did, mate, wouldn't miss you for the world.'

'Well, you've found me in some fucking state that's for sure. It's nearly the end and they've pumped enough drugs in me to fill a pharmacy. I'm going to leave this world on a morphine cloud after all. Twenty-odd years clean and I'm going to die stoned to the gills anyway.'

She laughed at her own gallows humour but a coughing fit cut her short.

'This is a sorry business, Luke, dying is really shit. I'd hoped I might last a little longer, get to see Emma become a doctor, maybe even see some grandchildren or something. I think I would've made a good grandma, don't you think? Instead my race is run at the ripe old age of 43. Poor Emma, she's only got Kate now. I think she'll be alright but I wish I could have been there for her for a little while longer. My poor baby girl, never had a father, now she's lost her mother and …'

She faded out in a drug haze, her face sweaty and unsettled. She wouldn't last long, that much was clear. I stayed by her bedside for a while, unsure of what else to do. She came to after a bit and began speaking again.

'Tell me your happy time, Luke.'

'My happy time?'

'Something, some moment that makes you happy, tell it to me.'

I thought for a moment before responding.

'Most Sundays I take my girls to the beach or the pool depending on the weather. We all have a big splash around for a couple of hours, then on the way home I get a roast chook from the supermarket and some bread and butter. We eat fresh hot chook wrapped in buttered bread at home while watching a Disney movie. Just me and my girls; it's something I look forward to all week, it's my happy time.'

She smiled a deep, happy smile and squeezed my hand affectionately.

'That's good Luke, you hang onto those moments, treasure them. Life is shorter than you think so hold on to those happy moments with your girls. We are here for such a short time so hold onto whatever happiness you can get.'

She faded out again and I thought to myself that if she fell asleep now I should probably go and leave her to it. Just as I was thinking this she came to again, her forehead bathed in sweat and her eyes trying to focus.

'Luke?'

'I'm here, mate.' I gave her my hand again to reassure her.

'Thank you for being my friend.'

'No worries, mate.'

She faded out again and I left her to rest.

I never spoke to her again. She died the next morning with Kate and Emma by her side.

The funeral was organised fairly quickly. Kate and Emma followed Beth's wishes. There was no mention of God or religion. A few people got up and spoke about what Beth meant to them and how much they would miss her. Emma got up and said that her mother had asked her to read a poem. It was *The Laughing Heart* by Charles Bukowski. Emma read it in a clear and confident voice. I felt every word of it.

Kate got up and spoke a few words. Then she said that Beth had requested a song be played. It was *The Everlasting* by Manic Street Preachers. We all listened in reverential silence.

The ceremony, such as it was, ended and the little gathering broke up. Beth was cremated and Kate and Emma took her ashes home.

I went home to Busselton and life went on. I was aware that something important had happened. A relationship, arguably the longest and most important one in my life, had ended. My best friend, arguably my only real friend, had died. I was more alone in the world than I had been before. The last little connection to my youth was gone.

I spent time with my wife and daughters. I remembered Beth's words and treasured every moment with my family, desperately capturing every happy memory I could.

I got a letter from Emma nearly six months after Beth died.

Dear Luke,

I wanted to write to you and say thank you for attending Mum's funeral and for being such a good friend to Mum through her life.

She told me all about the life you two had lived when you were young. Mum never censored or filtered anything for me, and I am so glad that you two were able to survive what you went through. To carve out a life for yourselves after so much trauma and misery is a real achievement.

In accordance with Mum's wishes, we have scattered her ashes at Marlo which is a little beach town on the coast of Victoria. Mum and Kate spent several happy holidays there and Mum wanted that to be her final resting place. We scattered her ashes on the beach and it felt really final. She really is gone forever, I have a hard time thinking that sometimes. I miss her so much.

I am still doing my medical studies. Mum was so proud of me when I got into university. She told me I was the first generation of her family to actually get in.

I am thinking about what sort of direction I will take with my career. I don't want to just chase money and be a doctor to rich housewives, etc. I want to make some sort of positive difference in the world. I have decided that I want to specialise in helping victims of sexual abuse. That way maybe some poor girl like my mum can be helped. That way Mum's life will have made a real difference.

I have enclosed something Mum wrote out that she wanted you to have. It is the Bukowski poem *The Laughing Heart*, the one I read out at the funeral. She wrote it out years ago, it meant a lot to her. She wanted you to have it. She said you would understand.

I don't have much more to say except thank you for being a good friend to my mum and I wish you and your family many years of happiness.

Yours Sincerely,

Emma.

I didn't know what to say to that so I never wrote back to her. I don't think she expected me to. She still had Kate and her studies and her friends at university to fill her life. She would be alright.

I put her letter away in a safe place. It was a Friday evening, I'd finished work for the week. I had a full weekend to spend with my wife and daughters. Some good moments ahead of me. Plenty of happiness to come, enough to make up for the grim years of my youth.

NIGHT SHIFT LAUGHS

Kenny woke up in the late afternoon and managed half a minute of feeling okay before reality hit him. Realising it was now fucked he got up and had a much needed piss before assessing what sort of day it was going to be.

He looked at his phone and saw that it was nearly quarter to five. That meant he'd managed to get about seven and a half hours sleep since he got home from the previous night's shift. He had one more to go tonight and then two days off. It was going to be a struggle.

He made a coffee and turned on the radio hoping to blank out his thoughts but it didn't work. He opened the messages on his phone knowing it would make him miserable.

There were no new ones, she'd kept her promise to stop speaking to him, so he re-read the old ones, the ones from a few days ago. They made him miserable and angry as he knew they would. She'd been so cold, he thought, did she have to be so cold about it? Couldn't she just have let him down gently?

There was no answer for him, and he realised time was passing and he needed to get ready, so he put the phone down for now.

He made himself something to eat, showered, shaved and got dressed in his work clothes without any real enthusiasm. He locked up and got in his car with a sense of utter misery and futility. As he drove he wondered where he'd gone wrong in life to find himself in this position.

Three-year relationship down the shitter because she thought she could do better, stuck in this shitty job doing nightshift most of the time because he couldn't get anything better and a growing sense that he was stuck, that he'd found his level in life and wouldn't move from it until he died.

He navigated his car through traffic and wished he was anywhere but here. He wished he could run away, instead of turning in to go to work, just get on the highway and keep driving, leave Adelaide, leave his life, follow the highway wherever it took him.

But he knew, even as he thought it, that he wouldn't do it. He had bills to pay, responsibilities to family and friends. He couldn't just decide "fuck it all" and leave. Yet he knew people who had; there was that young bloke who'd worked with them for a while last year, what was his name? Sandy? Samuel? Something like that. Anyway, he'd been a drifter, originally from Tasmania, he told stories of working on farms, picking fruit near Mildura, working at a resort near Cairns, surfing on the coast near Esperance. He'd just worked with them long enough to put together funds for the next adventure; he didn't give a shit about the job and despised those who did. Fucking suckholes, he used to say, imagine caring about a job like this. He despised the managers who thought they had achieved something by climbing up one rung on the ladder.

He left when he got enough money for more travel and they never heard from him again. Another person was hired to take his place and life went on. Kenny remained where he was.

He turned into the work carpark. It was always a depressing sight. A huge grey warehouse facility of one of the major supermarket chains. Trucks came in from farms and factories all over the country with produce. They received it and organised it overnight and the next day smaller trucks took it to various supermarkets all over Adelaide.

He hated the place. Every time he looked at it he felt a powerful urge to burn it down with everyone inside.

Despite the intense psychic pain it caused him, he got out of his car, went inside and clocked on.

At least it was a quiet night, he thought as he studied the distribution sheets. They could get this done without too much hassle and might get out at a reasonable hour. He looked at who was with him tonight. Danny, he was alright; Carter, he was okay as well. His heart sank when he saw Tom's name. Tom was a suckhole and he strongly suspected that he was telling tales to the boss to curry favour. Angus was on and he felt himself smile at the thought; Angus was still young, probably a pot head or just an irresponsible skater kid who didn't give a fuck. Either way Angus was fun, always managed to make everyone laugh at some point during the night.

He headed to the dock and got on with it. The first truck came in and they started unloading it, their bodies and muscles getting into the rhythm of work. Angus was already talking shit and getting a chuckle out of Danny. Tom glared at him and continued putting in conspicuous effort into stacking pallets as if he would be rewarded for it.

They had a gap between the second and third trucks and that was when Angus came out with it.

'Hey Kenny, check this out.'

He pulled out his phone and showed Kenny some stupid video. It was a meme-mashup thing based on the Lord of Rings movies. There was a stupid but catchy electronic beat and the bit where the elf guy says "They're taking the Hobbits to Isengard" repeated on some sort of loop.

It was utterly stupid and hilarious. Kenny had a good laugh.

'Check this out, there's a ten-hour version.'

'Why the fuck would anyone make a ten-hour version of that shit?'

'Nah, it's like a meme challenge; people try and sit there and watch the whole ten hours just for a laugh.'

'Sounds like people with no job.'

'How mad would it be if I put on the dock sound system?' Angus had a cheeky, malicious smile on his face and it occurred to Kenny to realise just how alive this young bloke was.

He hesitated for a minute and then decided to hell with it.

'Go on, just for a laugh.'

Angus gave a manic little chuckle and raced off to the control panel in the office. Carter saw him go and asked Kenny what the young bloke was up to.

'You'll see.' A few seconds later the idiotic tune came over the speakers in the dock.

Angus came out of the office in triumphant glee.

'Ten-hour version, cunts, *They're Taking the Hobbits to Isengard*! Mad tunes for work!'

Danny and Carter laughed at him.

'You're fucking cooked Angus; what the fuck is this shit?'

'Bro, it's our new soundtrack for the loading dock, this is our motherfucking JAM tonight!'

They laughed some more.

'Is that all it says? Taking the Hobbits to Isengard? That's it? The whole song?' Carter asked.

'Yep, ten hours bro! Just go with it, vibe out and bounce a little at work, have some fun.'

Angus had got them all laughing. He was good for that.

Another truck came in, they began to unload. The driver heard the song playing over the system and looked confused.

'What the fuck is this shit?'

'Young fella thinks it's funny, we're humouring him.' Kenny replied while he signed the paperwork.

The driver looked over at young Angus doing the boogie while he pushed a trolley jack. He was singing along now much to the amusement of Carter and Danny.

'Cunt's cooked,' was the driver's diagnosis. He left them to it.

They organised more pallets and put them in their places ready to go tomorrow. All the while the idiotic song played over the speakers. Kenny was beginning to like it. It certainly made the night a bit more fun.

Another truck came and was unloaded. They laughed and sang along to the stupid meme song as they worked, it's silliness making the night go faster and more pleasantly.

In between the trucks Angus danced along and joked around. Everyone enjoyed it, except for Tom. Miserable bastard refused to join in and Kenny was surer than ever that he was telling tales to the bosses.

At length they got the last truck unloaded, pallets organised and everything ready for the day crew in the morning. Kenny looked at the time on his phone and realised they'd managed to get everything done in very good time. They could knock off a little early with a clear conscience.

Angus took his phone back and the music stopped.

'Thank fuck for that!' Carter yelled with a laugh.

'Bro, I'll make a special playlist just for you,' Angus responded, smiling. Everyone was happy, everyone felt good, this was abnormal but a welcome development.

Angus asked Kenny for a ride home and Kenny agreed. They all clocked off and headed for the carpark.

Kenny drove towards where Angus lived, the dawn just threatening to break. Angus was telling him some story about bringing home a "skatepark slut" and nearly getting busted by his Mum. He dropped Angus off and headed for home, the breakfast radio show chattering away quietly and not disturbing his mild happiness.

He got home and slept. A solid eight hours. It didn't matter because he had the next couple of days off. He vaguely thought about what he was going to do with the days. He felt like going to the pool or something active. Do him good, he thought, bit of exercise and fresh air.

He checked his emails while he had his second coffee and was a bit more awake. There was one from work.

"Attention all staff: Music is not to be played over the loading docks sound system. This sound system is for work related announcements and emergency notifications only. Thank you, Management."

A bitterness flooded his soul. Fucking Tom had been telling tales again. The pathetic little suckhole thinking he was going to get promoted because he dobbed on people.

Kenny thought about his days off. They were ruined now, like someone had shat in his ice cream. He sat in bitter silence and drank his coffee.

OVER PEBBLES AND SAND

Every Sunday afternoon they play chess at the Port Lincoln Public Library.

You can see them arrive just after the Library opens at 1.00, mostly on foot or on pushbikes. Men for the most part, middle aged or older, slightly worn and moth-eaten in appearance, making haste for the sliding doors at the side of the building. If a keen observer was to watch them he would notice a telling thing in their body language. When they are still outside on the street walking towards the Library they exhibit what a body language expert would call "signs of submission". They walk with their heads mostly bowed, their shoulders drooping, avoiding eye contact with other people on the street. All the classic signs of people who have been beaten badly by life.

And yet, the moment they enter those sliding doors their faces light up, a burden is lifted from their shoulders. They're in a safe and happy place.

The Librarians have set up several tables at one end of the Library with chess sets. This is a regular Sunday afternoon thing. They gather in their little area of the Library for fellowship and lighthearted competition and a respite from the cold, lonely world outside.

Theodore, known to one and all as Ted, is nearly always here first. He is an older gentleman, worn down by the hard turns of life and almost completely alone in the world. He needs his Sunday afternoons more than he could ever explain. He gets in early, says hello to the Librarian and sits down in front of a chess set waiting for someone else to come and play. With his grey hair slicked back and his mouldy cardigan looking worse under the lights of the Library he looks like an older, worn and malnourished version of Bob Hawke.

Peter, known as Clarky because his surname is Clarke, arrives next, usually on his pushbike. He is younger than Ted but life has not been kind to him either and the signs of age, poverty and loneliness are written on his face for all to see. He is so tanned his skin looks like leather, the legacy of years spent working on fishing boats. There are almost certainly Melanomas lurking in that tan, waiting for their chance to blossom forth like cancerous roses.

Clarky greets Ted with a smile that is gratefully returned. Ted hasn't actually spoken to another human being for three days prior to this so Clarky's cheery hello is like fresh water to a man dying of thirst in the desert. Clarky sits across from Ted and they begin a game and make lighthearted chat.

Charles arrives a few minutes later, also on pushbike. He greets Ted and Clarky but sits a few seats down from them to await other players. Charles and Clarky share an uneasy vibe. They both attend the two Alcoholics Anonymous meetings in Port Lincoln and they both used to work on fishing boats before the drink, old age, their battered bodies and their bad reputations as drunks took that source of income. Not being qualified for much else they almost immediately fell into poverty from which neither has managed yet to escape.

They see each other twice a week at the AA meetings and then again at the Library on Sundays. They also remember each other from back in the day on fishing boats when life was one long drunken good time and they had no idea they'd one day be broke and alone and going to the Library on Sunday to play chess because they desperately need the human contact.

Clarky thinks of this often. He wishes he could get a time machine and go back to talk to his younger self. Tell himself to stop drinking, stop being a young wastrel, either get off the fishing boats into a steady job or else bank the money he made while he can. He wishes he could make his younger self understand how quickly a person can go from being a carefree young bloke cashed up from a good tuna season with plenty of mates to drink with, to being broke and alone, body worn out from years of abuse, social life reduced to two AA meetings a week and chess at the Library on Sundays.

Charles also struggles with the decline in his life. He had hopes that he could get some compensation money for his bad back from the tuna company but the lawyer told him he didn't have a case. Charles often thinks about how long he has left to live and what he can reasonably expect from whatever is left of his life. For a long time he has kept up the hope that he could find some way out of the fate he has found himself in. When he got sober in AA he thought that would solve most of the problems but to his dismay he discovered that stopping drinking prevents one particular type of catastrophe but does nothing to prevent a general slow slide into poverty, loneliness and despair.

Young Tom arrives and greets everyone. He is far younger than the others, still in high school in fact, but equally lonely. He is a nerdy young man, could easily pass for the nerd in one of those American campus comedy films of the 1980s. Shy and quietly spoken, he sits down across from Charles and they begin a rather competitive game.

The Librarian walks past them and smiles. She feels a warmth towards them; the Sunday chess sessions were her idea, Libraries as Community spaces and all that, one must keep up with the times. She also knows the grim reality of funding. The more people who walk through the door and make the little sensor click over the more likely they are to maintain their current funding levels and maybe even raise them a little. This little gathering of lonely men playing chess on Sundays combined with the usual Sunday afternoon traffic is probably enough for them to keep a staff member on.

Games finish and the players swap around challenging different opponents. A few random new people join in for a game or two.

Young Tom finds himself playing Ted. He enjoys games with Ted. The quality of play is so much better and Ted takes an interest in him. The feeling is mutual. Ted looks forward to his games with Tom and even more so enjoys a chat with him. Tom doesn't know this but Ted was once a school teacher of a sort and a very educated man. In fact he had been so highly regarded amongst the education profession that he had briefly advised the State Government on education policy.

Of course, that was a long time ago, before everything fell apart, before life became a long and lonely thing to be endured.

But Ted still feels that old passion for learning and education somewhere inside him and it finds an outlet in his paternal concern for young Tom's future.

'Ready for your exams?'

'Yeah, I think so. Did a practice one online and did really well so hopefully the real one goes as easily.'

'Have you made a decision about university?'

'I still really want to go to The University of Adelaide but Flinders has the same courses and it's easier to get in. It depends what my final scores are I guess. I'm going to apply for the scholarship to Sydney University as well but it's a long shot.'

'Why Sydney University?'

'To get as far away from Port Lincoln as possible.'

The bitterness in his voice gives him away and Ted feels real pity and compassion for the boy. Being a smart and bookish kid in a country town school full of meathead footy players can't be fun. The bullying, the loneliness; no wonder Tom wants to go as far away as he can. Ted wishes with all his heart for the boy to get his scholarship and go to Sydney to seek his fortune but at the same time knows he will miss him coming to play chess every Sunday. The closest thing I have to a friend, Ted thinks sadly. The sadness of the thought hurts. He debates asking Tom to write to him when he goes but he worries it'll sound creepy and pathetic and besides, do young people even know how to write letters anymore?

The afternoon stretches on. More games are played, players swap around, chat and laugh. There is real warmth and camaraderie around these tables in the corner of the Library. Real human warmth, the thing that they really come for. When all is said and done, the chess is incidental.

The Library closes at 4.00 and the men wander out. Even in the closing up of the Library their social isolation is obvious. At the check-out machines there are mums with kids checking out books for the week. Walking past them, unnoticed and unloved by anyone, are the lonely men who came to play chess.

Once outside the door defeat settles down on them again. They say goodbye to each other and promise to see each other again next week before going their separate ways. Clarky leaves on his pushbike, young Tom is picked up by his Mum, Charles drives off in his old Astra that's nearly ready to die while Ted slowly walks home.

The brisk wind coming off the bay flicks Ted's grey hair around and he thinks that when his pension comes in on Thursday he'll go get a haircut. That's something to look forward to, he thinks, I can have a good chat with that nice bloke at the barber's. He knows that is probably the only human conversation he's likely to have until next Sunday.

He decides to take the long way home and walk along the foreshore. He wants to delay the moment of entering his empty place as long as possible. He walks along the beach as the sun is going down. How I dearly wish I was not here, he thinks to himself, as the prospect of a long and lonely week stretches ahead of him like a tomb.

THE COUNTRY ELECTORATE

Gary Treloar was having a bad day. The chief whip of the South Australian Liberal Party had just told him he would have to resign. He stared at his very expensive steak dinner in disbelief.

'Resign? Isn't that a tad drastic? A little bit overboard? Surely there's another way?'

The Chief Whip, Robert Pendleton, shook his head sadly but firmly.

'Sorry Gary, this comes from the top, there's a state election in just over six months and the Premier doesn't want an easy target for the opposition to latch onto. You fucked up, even you know that. This close to an election fuck ups are not tolerated.'

He shrugged his shoulders as if to say that was it.

'I admitted the mistake,' Gary continued, 'and publicly stated that I was paying the money back. That should be enough, shouldn't it? The media will have moved on in a week or so, you know how fickle the public are. Some footballer will be caught doing coke off a hooker's arse next week and nobody will remember I did anything. After all I've done for the party and all the wins I've got for my electorate, I make one fuck up and it's see you later, Gary. Really?'

Pendleton laid his fork beside his overpriced pasta and looked squarely at Gary.

'Nobody's throwing you on the scrapheap, Gary. You don't need to panic. A position has been arranged for you.'

'A position?'

'You remember those roadworks and highway improvements you announced last year? Big win for your electorate and for the government. Well, the company that won the contract is willing to take you on as a consultant. Handsome salary and nice perks. More importantly, you're going to be the go-to man between the government and the company. The Premier wants more roadworks, he likes announcing them, they play well with the electorate and they win votes. The Premier wants someone in the company who can make sure things are completed on time and on budget and the company wants someone who can talk to the Premier about new contracts and make sure the tender process works in their favour.'

'That would be your role, Gary. You'd be a very popular man with the government and the company. What do you say?'

By the end of Robert's little speech Gary was actually smiling. The news that had ruined his dinner was now of little consequence. Greener pastures awaited.

'That doesn't sound so bad. I could be very useful in that role and of course, I do love roadworks.'

'We all love roadworks, Gary, they're a fucking winner on every level.'

Gary lifted his beer in salute. 'Then here's to roadworks. May we announce many more in the years to come.'

Pendleton lifted his own beer and clinked glasses with Gary.

'Fuck yeah, viva fucking roadworks and the votes they bring in.'

William Little wasn't happy either.

'Why the seat of Flinders? It's a safe Liberal seat and has been forever. I have no chance of winning it. You're wasting my talents on a lost cause.'

James Teakin, one of the heavyweights of the South Australian Labor Party, was tempted to say something unkind about the "talents" of William Little but restrained himself in the interests of the party.

'Listen William, this is one of those "paying your dues" type of things. Everyone has to go through it. We know you're not going to win, that's not the point. The point is to give it your best shot, show that you've got some real fight in you. Do good on this, put in the hard yards, show us you're a fighter, and next time you get a winnable seat. Shit, if you actually increase the Labor vote a tiny bit you might even get a safe seat. And from there bigger things might open up to you but only if you show us that you're a real party man.'

'I've been a party man since I was a teenager in Young Labor.' William hurriedly assured him.

'Good, so "William Little, Labor for Flinders" is what the signs will read. Give it a red hot go and do the best you can, that's all we're asking. Now, about your grandfather? Have you asked him yet? Is he willing? He'd be a real asset.'

'Not yet, I'll go see him tomorrow.'

'Good man. Tell him I said hello.'

Gary Treloar would normally be a bit miffed about being forced to announce his own successor. However, he'd had several meetings with the company he would soon be working for and the potential of the job had made him almost enthusiastic about no longer being an MP.

His successor was Todd Newman, former Mayor of Cummins, livestock dealer and a proper good old boy. The party had decided "more of the same" was the way to go and that's what the electorate of Flinders was going to get.

Gary had given a speech about his legacy and how great the Eyre Peninsula was and how he intended to serve the community in another capacity. Todd had come on and given a speech about the great future that awaited the Eyre Peninsula and the wonderful opportunities the future held.

Gary thought it was a great speech. Bloody should be, he thought, I gave the exact same one when I was first elected.

The Liberal Party faithful of Port Lincoln and surrounds were gathered for the event and applauded. Everything was going smoothly. As the speeches were finished and the gathering dissolved into informal chats, Gary smiled, God I fucking love roadworks, he thought. The more the better.

William Little was somewhat intimidated by his grandfather. John Little was a rock of a man; not so much physically intimidating, more of a moral force that impressed you when you spoke to the man. He'd been a Labor man back in the day when that meant something. He'd stood on picket lines and been bashed by cops. He'd marched in anti-Vietnam War protests and been bashed by cops. He'd protested uranium mines and been bashed by cops.

By contrast William had never broken a law or been to a protest in his life and found himself sweating and nervous whenever the police pulled him over for an RBT.

John Little's most impressive achievement, and the reason William had been asked to speak with him, was being a backbencher in the Whitlam government back in the day. John Little had entered Parliament in 1972 on the wave of hope and optimism of the Whitlam moment and left in 1977 in despair and defeat.

'Hello Grandad, how's things?'

William always overdid the chirpy and cheerful introductions where his grandfather was concerned. He couldn't help it. The man made him nervous.

'Young William, and what are you up to today?'

Without asking, John made them both a cup of tea; strong, scalding hot and with barely any sugar or milk, the way he preferred it and something William had never got the hang of.

He set William's mug in front of him and sat down opposite in his ancient chair that could have passed for a throne of some decrepit king.

'What's the news of the world, my boy?'

'I've been selected for the seat of Flinders, Grandad; I'm going to be the Labor candidate at the next state election.'

John snorted dismissively and William shrank again.

'Waste of bloody time if you ask me.'

'Well yes, it's a safe Liberal seat but if I put up a good fight I might get a winnable seat next time.'

'I meant being a Labor candidate at all is a waste of bloody time.'

William wasn't sure how to answer. There was an awkward silence for a few minutes before William mustered up the courage to ask the question he'd come here to ask.

'Grandad, I've been asked to ask you something.'

'And here it is, the purpose of the visit.'

'Some people in the party would like you to come out and endorse me. Maybe be seen at a few events, that sort of thing.'

'Why me?'

'Because you're one of the last of the Whitlam generation. That's how we're going to present it, "The last of Whitlam's Lions, still fighting the good fight," that sort of thing.'

'Gough never referred to anyone as a "Lion" in my hearing. I don't know where you got that one from.'

'It's something they worked out in the focus groups.'

'Focus groups?' John erupted 'Fucking focus groups? This is what you do now?'

William winced.

'If the Labor Party is using focus groups to gauge the mood of the people, then it is truly lost. Once upon a time we were the workers' party, by the workers, of the workers and for the workers. What are you now? What do you stand for William? Who are you? Do you even know?'

The old man's voice thundered like some Old Testament Prophet while William shriveled into the couch.

'What is the point of the Labor Party today? What is it working towards? When I was in it we had a vision, an idea of what society should look like, that's what we were fighting for. What are you fighting for William? A better society or just your own career? That's the problem, it's all just career people now, nobody believes in anything, they just want to make a career for themselves. The movement used to be full of principled amateurs, the cream of the working class. Now it's professionals with no principles, the dregs of the middle class, ambitious mediocrities every one of them.'

'You are my grandson, William, and it pains me to say this but that's what you are, an ambitious mediocrity. By rights you should be working for an insurance company. That's about your level of competence, mid-level management in an insurance company. You could have a perfectly decent life like that, maybe even do a little bit of good in the world coaching your kids footy on the weekends or something. But no, you've got delusions of grandeur like the rest of them. You think you're going to be a somebody in politics. I bet you practice Churchill speeches in the mirror, don't you? You believe that by playing the party politics game you'll be important one day but you are a mediocrity William and no pre-selection for a safe seat is ever going to change that.'

The old man sat back in his chair and sipped his tea.

'So you don't want to come to some party events?' William asked from the back of his chair.

The old man glared at him across his mug of tea.

The ABC was covering the South Australian State Election as it always did. Anyone who cared enough to watch their coverage saw the numbers rolling in from each seat and the talking heads discussing it.

The presenter interrupted one of the talking heads with an update.

'And I'll just have to stop you there for a moment, Antony Green has some updated results from the seat of Flinders, I believe ...'

BROTHERS, COUSINS AND NIECES

They're a funny lot my family. The Mollenberg family, as South Australian as it's possible to be. Not that being super-South Australian has ever done us any good, it's not like the Premier came out and gave us some award for it or anything. We were poor white trash when we first got off the boat 180 years ago and we've managed not to advance our situation very much in the intervening years.

You can probably guess from the name that our origins are German. Our family were part of that big exodus of Lutherans who left Germany in the 1840s and came to South Australia. There are traces of that migration all over the state if you know what you're looking for; Germanic sounding place names, Germanic sounding surnames and people who look like recruitment ads for the Hitler Youth.

You'll find all of these in the little country towns of South Australia, the places that most people only drive through or fly over on their way to somewhere else.

There's a strong Cornish line in my family, too. The Cornish immigrants who settled on the Yorke Peninsula to mine copper and build a life for their families managed, at multiple points in the family history, to intermarry with my lot. Hence we tend to look a bit less "Germanic" than some other families. What's the best way to describe us? Well, if you can picture those Nazi propaganda pictures of the ideal Aryan specimen but make the hair a sort of dusty, dirty blonde rather than the gold-blonde they preferred, then give the face a kind of gone to seed, bumpkin look, add in a fondness for rum and fornication, and that's a good basic picture of my family.

We're spread out all over the State now but most of us have held on in the little towns of the Eyre Peninsula, the Yorke Peninsula and the mid-North, clinging on to these tiny little places like the last sentries of a forgotten and defeated army.

I grew up in these places, moved around a little bit when I was young because my father had to move for work. I hated them when I was young. I was so desperate to escape that life. I fled to Adelaide in the hope of making something of myself. Of course, it didn't work out. Why would it? Why would the modern world make a space for a white trash shitbag from the bush like me? I always felt just a little "off" when I was trying to get ahead in the city, just a little unbalanced and behind the eight ball. I didn't speak the language the successful people spoke, I didn't have the right mentality, I didn't understand the rules of the game that I was trying to win. I had no chance really.

After six and a half years of struggling in the city, six and a half years of failure and humiliation and poverty, I gave up and went home to my dad. He was living in Port Augusta at the time. He had a job with the contractors doing highway repairs. I moved in with him and got a job at the local bottle shop for lack of better options. After a few months he lent me the money to go do some training courses, truck licence, bobcat and excavator tickets, things like that. After a few months more and with his help I was able to turn these tickets into a job in a mine in Western Australia.

I got hooked on the money that you can get in the mining game. Hooked as well on the rootless, casual lifestyle of a fly in/fly out worker. For me Perth was a liberation, nobody knew me or my family there. I had no roots, no identity, just another cashed up bogan in a Hi-Vis shirt. It was great.

Unfortunately, the mining game is prone to instability. Some arsehole on the stock exchange decides he's not willing to pay as much for whatever commodity you're digging out of the ground and boom! The mine closes or cuts staff and you're furiously emailing off resumés again.

After a decade of this I was tired again. Have you ever noticed how tired you are all the time as an adult? Or is that just me? It's like once you're past 21 everything just becomes an exhausting grind and all you want is a couple extra hours sleep, please for the love of God just a couple hours more sleep.

I felt the need for home and family again. Perhaps I was just getting old.

I rang my cousin Paul and asked him if I could crash for a while in the granny flat of his place in Port Lincoln. I didn't have a plan as such, I just wanted to be around family again, settle things down a bit and rest.

Paul was my cousin on my dad's side, same surname and everything. We even looked fairly similar. My Auntie Kelly, my dad's sister, told me once that Paul was actually my half-brother. She claimed that my father and his mother had a quick fling on the sly during which Paul was conceived. I didn't know if I should believe Auntie Kelly or not. She was a narky old bag who loved gossip and lived for the dirt of other people's lives but she had a worrying tendency to be more right than wrong when it came to what people were up to.

Paul and I had grown up together. We'd remained close in adulthood although our lives were completely different. Paul had never left the little town life he'd grown up with. He felt no need to strive for something better or different. He was happy with his lot.

He'd chased money for a while when he was young. Working on fishing boats out of Port Lincoln, he'd spent a couple years with the Tuna Fleet, long stints at sea for big money. He'd settled down a bit when he met his missus. Her name was Nadine; she was a Kiwi, working behind the bar at one of the local pubs at the time. They'd shacked up together, she got pregnant and they got married.

Their oldest child, Courtney, was thirteen now, a moody teenager but basically a good kid. She was an odd mix; she had the Germanic-Cornish look about her face and head from our side of the family but the drop of Maori blood from her mother gave her long straight hair that was the same colour as a crow's feathers. She looked quite haunting. Sometimes, when she stared at you, she looked like a witch out of some medieval folk tale.

I arrived in Port Lincoln at the end of February. I settled in with Paul. We had a drink together the first night I was there and did all the usual catch-up chatting. Courtney sat up with us for a while and listened to our talk of family and old times. Nadine eventually told her she had to go to bed because she had school in the morning. As Paul and I talked I felt the warmth of family and home again. The feeling of belonging to a place and a tribe. Or perhaps it was just the rum warming my bones.

'Jackie boy, it's good to have you home again.'

Paul expressed his affection in that awkward half-drunk way that men do because they don't know how else to say things.

The next day I set about finding a job in Port Lincoln. I figured I was going to be here for a couple of months at least so I needed something to keep me going. It took me about an hour before I got a job at the bottle shop of the Northern Hotel. Good old bottle shops, the standby employment option of so many people, like the dole but with less paperwork and more money.

I fell into the routine so easy it was as though I was destined for it. I'd do four or five shifts at the bottle shop each week, sometimes more if we were short of bodies. In my time off I'd mostly hang around with Paul and talk shit over beer.

'Whatever happened to young David?'

'David from High School?'

'No, Auntie Rita's kid.'

'Dave wasn't Auntie Rita's kid; he was her stepson.'

'Yeah well, anyway, what happened to him? Haven't heard from him in years.'

'He's a full-time carer for Rita now, she's got the fucking Alzheimer's or whatever you call it. Not long for this world.'

'Shit.'

'Yeah, I doubt it'll be a big funeral when the time comes, Rita managed to upset everyone in the family. Half of them haven't spoken to her in years.'

'So how come her stepson puts up with her and cares for her?'

'Word is there's a very nice surprise for him in her will. That house of hers in Reynella.'

'The plot thickens.'

'It always does.'

On and on like that we'd go as we sipped our beers. A couple of old blokes talking about our family and days gone by. It occurred to me that we'd become the old blokes we remembered from our own childhoods. You grow up being bored by the rambling stories of your older relatives then when you're older you start telling your own rambling stories: the circle of life and all that.

Courtney sometimes sat with us as we drank our beers and talked our bullshit. She seemed interested in our family sagas and gossip or maybe she had nothing better to do. Because I was working bottle shop hours and was often off work during the day, she'd bludge a ride into town with me.

'Uncle Jack, can you give me a ride to the skate park?'

'Uncle Jack, can you give me a ride to the foreshore, please?'

I didn't mind too much. She was a good kid and being around youthful vigour made me feel a little bit more alive, as though I'd absorbed some of it via osmosis. I'd watch her and her friends at the skate park for a few minutes after I'd dropped her off. To be young again, I'd think, and reluctantly pull out and drive home.

I felt comfortable in my little groove and had no real plans so I decided to get some accommodation that was a little bit more permanent. I rented a place on Dublin Street just before the crest of the hill. It was more comfortable and I was able to get my stuff out of storage and settle in a bit more.

I had an ulterior motive for wanting my own pad. I'd caught the eye of one of the bar girls at the Northern. Her name was Marissa, local girl, hay-coloured hair and a bum that looked great in jeans. We'd got friendly at work and then started hanging out a little. When I got my own place she started visiting, then staying the night. Within a few months we were a pretty solid couple.

July came around. I got my tax return done and banked the money. Paul did the same with his. He suggested one day that we go visit my dad. My dad was living in Spalding then, a little town in the Mid-North that wasn't much but he seemed happy there. Paul's idea was that we drive over and see him, stay a couple of days, then pop down to the city for a day or two and do a bunch of shopping before driving home to Port Lincoln again.

I was keen so we organised time off from our jobs.

It was September before we actually did it. We left it that late partly on account of Courtney. She nagged her Dad to come with us and Paul agreed, which meant we had to organise the trip around school holidays. A few weeks before we were due to go, Paul told me that he and Nadine were expecting another baby, their fifth. He told me the news with a sheepish kind of half grin on his face. I took that to mean this baby wasn't planned.

Marissa had more or less moved in with me by this point. She was starting to drop hints about taking things to a more serious level. Constantly not-so-casually mentioning that various people she knew had got married or were planning a family. That sort of deeply unsubtle feminine hint. I made the mistake of telling her about Paul and Nadine's little surprise and it rubbed her the right way.

'Awww that's really romantic and beautiful though, like they're just in love and a baby just happens, you know? It's like they're just leaving themselves open to whatever and trusting in life.'

I knew damn well what she was thinking and later that night I felt her arm for her birth control implant before we had sex. Never take chances around a broody female.

The day we set off for Spalding was sunny and cheerful. Courtney was slightly disorganised and Nadine had to yell at her a couple of times until she got all her shit together but eventually we got on the road. We took my car. I had only bought it a year ago so we figured it was less likely to break down than Paul's, and the highway flowed smoothly under the wheels.

Paul occupied himself with flicking through the radio trying to find a station that didn't annoy him while Courtney alternated between fiddling around on her phone, looking blankly out the window and eventually, when we were out of phone signal range, picking up a book and reading.

We stopped at Port Augusta for lunch and we managed to get to Spalding about mid-afternoon.

We pulled into the little town and I was struck by how familiar it was. I had grown up in towns like this all over the state. Wheat and sheep towns with an old pub, a little district hall and a small shop and not much else. Full of people like my dad and me, full of families like mine, the leftover white trash relics of an Australia that was supposed to have died years ago but somehow has managed to hang on.

We pulled up at my dad's house. It was an old stone place on the very edge of the little town, built in the 1920s and barely changed in all that time. Dad was happy to see us and laughed and joked with us all as we got our stuff out of the car and settled into the spare room. Before very long beers were pulled out of the fridge and passed around. Dad jokingly offered one to Courtney and when she over-eagerly went to accept it he called her a ratbag and told Paul he'd have to watch her.

We drank and talked through what was left of the afternoon and eventually Dad nominated me to be cook for the night. I made us all a big mess of spag bol and the beers kept flowing as we ate. Paul and Dad seemed to get on better than I ever remembered. As I watched them I remembered what Auntie Kelly had told me and I thought that they really did look more like father and son than uncle and nephew.

I flaked out a couple of hours after eating. Courtney made her way to bed a little while after. Paul stayed up with Dad talking shit and drinking beer until I don't know what hour. I didn't hear him come in. At some point in the night Paul let out a fart that seemed to go on forever and was loud enough to wake Courtney and me.

'Jesus, dad you're disgusting,' Courtney muttered before rolling over and going back to sleep.

I was first awake but Courtney stirred shortly after and joined me for a cuppa on the back porch as the sun struggled to rise above the horizon. Like all teenagers she couldn't just appreciate the serenity, she wanted to know what we were going to do today.

'Your father ever take you shooting?'

'No, Mum made him sell his guns years ago. She said she didn't want them with us kids in the house.'

'Of course, do you want to come shooting with me today? See if we can bag a fox or two?'

She was keen so I led her to the shed and opened up my dad's gun safe. The code was my birthday conveniently enough. I took out the old Remington .223 that had been designated as my rifle when I was young although it was registered in my father's name.

I took a box of ammo and dug around the shed until I found the old army camo jackets stashed away in a box full of miscellaneous wires. I put one on and so did Courtney. Hers was several sizes too big and swallowed her up. She looked like a child playing dress ups.

We went back to the house and gathered a backpack full of muesli bars and bottled water. I wrote a note for the sleepers, telling them where we had gone and left it on the kitchen table. Then Courtney followed me as I headed out the back and casually climbed the fence into the neighbouring farmland.

'Won't we get in trouble for going on this person's land?'

'Nah they're friends with Dad and he has blanket permission to go on their land and shoot foxes. We've done it before, they know us.'

Reassured, she followed me across the dusty paddock in the general direction of the distant tree line, the wheat stubble crunching under our feet.

I found us a spot amongst some trees facing towards a gully overgrown with scrub. We lay down on our bellies and I put the backpack in front of me to rest the rifle on. I got the whistle out of my jacket pocket.

'Watch this. Stay still and quiet.'

Courtney nodded as I put the whistle to my lips and blew. The sound, mimicking a lamb in distress pierced the serenity of the countryside. I blew several times, spacing each blow by a couple of minutes to make it seem more natural the way Dad had taught me.

Sure enough, after a few minutes a fox appeared, cautiously sticking its head out of the scrubby gully. Courtney tensed beside me. She'd obviously seen it too but, good kid that she was, was staying silent like I'd told her to.

I lined up the rifle, carefully watching through the scope and controlling my breathing as the fox looked around trying to locate the lamb in distress.

The shot made Courtney jump and the fox tumbled over on itself, struck firm on its proud chest. I carefully worked the bolt, discharging the spent casing and loading another round in the chamber.

'Let's go take a look at him.'

Courtney nodded, still a little rattled from the violence of the shot, and we stood up and walked towards the gully.

The fox lay on its back as if it had just received terrible news and fainted from the shock. There was a nice clean bullet hole in its chest. I'd hit it good and true.

'You got him good, Uncle Jack,' Courtney said in awe.

I couldn't help but feel a little bit proud of myself.

'C'mon, we'll try the other little gully over this way a bit.'

Courtney followed me as we left the corpse for the crows and headed towards the next spot. Once there we set ourselves up as before only this time I let Courtney take the rifle and assume the shooting position. I showed her how it worked, how to squeeze the trigger correctly and how to work the bolt. I took up a spot just next to her and started blowing with the whistle.

It took a little while longer this time but a fox appeared and left the cover of the gully scrub to make himself a tempting target for us. Perhaps too tempting, Courtney fired way too early and missed completely. The fox bolted back into the scrub, never to be seen again.

'Too soon, Courtney, he's halfway down his burrow by now. We won't see him again.'

'I thought I had him lined up, Uncle Jack.'

'Thought you did and actually did are two different things sweetheart, but that's alright. We'll try again further up the way.'

We walked off to try again. Over the next hour or two we tried several spots but had no more luck. Either we had exhausted the fox population of the area or, more likely, we had made too much noise with the first two shots and they'd gone to ground. We decided to sit down under a shady tree and eat our muesli bars for morning tea.

This is one of those things I missed when I lived in the city. Finding a quiet spot somewhere and just enjoying the silence. A few birds in the background, the wind in the trees and aside from that, nothing. It's heavenly. We sipped our water bottles and chewed our muesli bars underneath an old gum tree that must have been at least eighty-years old. The sun was properly up by now and the sky was that vivid blue colour you only get in the bush. Here and there a bird flitted across a vast canvas of unbroken blue that made you aware of your own smallness.

I noted with silent approval that Courtney didn't unnecessarily break the peace and quiet. Some kids that age just have to talk for the sake of talking. I disapprove of noisy people; it shows a lack of character and intelligence in my opinion, so I was happy she was able to just appreciate the serenity.

While I was musing on this I saw it.

A feral cat, big bastard, came skulking along through the stubble maybe a hundred metres away from us. I tapped Courtney on the leg and indicated for her to be silent while I gathered up the rifle as quietly as I could. I didn't have time to build up a good shooting position so I just rested my free arm on my knee as I squatted and mounted the rifle into the crook of my elbow. I controlled my breathing and got my aim correct.

I pulled the trigger and the cat dropped like a sack of potatoes to the ground, hit clean through its shoulder.

We walked up to look at the carcass.

The hole was neat and perfect through its shoulder blade. It had never known what hit it. It was a large cat, a dusty colour the way true feral cats all are, strong and powerful like a miniature lion.

'I've never seen a cat like that, Uncle Jack. It's big.'

'These feral cats that have been out in the bush for generations get like this, natural selection and all that. The weak ones get weeded out of the gene pool and the biggest, meanest bastards survive to breed the next generation. When I was working in the mines in WA we used to see them hanging around the camp. Huge, bigger than this, but always that same dusty colour to blend in with the bush and the dirt.'

I thought for a moment about the wild nowhere I'd spent years of my life working in. The vast empty centre of Australia, full of nothing but dust and heartbreak. I remembered empty, disused and abandoned mining camps, places shut down when the economic winds shifted direction; places taken over again by the desert wildlife, havens for snakes, crows, wild dogs and feral cats.

'One day when we're all gone and our civilization has collapsed, these feral cats will still be out here, only then they'll be free to wander into whatever ruins of our towns and cities are left. By that time natural selection will have made them even bigger and meaner than they are now. They'll be like tigers, dusty, dirty Australian tigers, wandering over our graves. They'll have the last laugh over us, nothing surer.'

Courtney looked at me a little funny. I realised my mind had wandered and I'd gone a little bit over the top.

'You're a bit weird sometimes, Uncle Jack.'

We left the cat's carcass and trudged back home, both of us now hungry.

Dad and Paul were awake by now and Paul was cooking up a big old-fashioned fry up breakfast under Dad's watchful eye and critical direction.

'The great white hunters have returned! Get anything?'

I told Dad about the foxes and the cat as he listened and nodded.

'The foxes in this district have been getting worse the last few years, not enough shooters to keep their numbers down. Old Tony Hyden, you remember Tony, don't you? He lost a quarter of his lambs to foxes a few years ago. He wanted to drop 1080 baits all over his property but the Greenies in the city have changed the rules and you can't do that now. Cats are getting bad, too. There was one lurking around here last winter. I reckon it must have been a female with kittens nearby, big bastard of a thing too. Wouldn't have liked to try and catch it alive, reckon it would've fought like a lion.'

I nodded in agreement as Paul dumped plates loaded with bacon, beans, eggs and toast in front of Courtney and me. Courtney began to demolish her food; I followed her lead, discovering that I was hungrier than I thought.

Paul and Dad chatted a little, slightly seedy from the beers of the night before but still cheerful and alive. Dad got to talking about his latest project car as Courtney and I finished our breakfast. Dad had been doing up old cars ever since Mum died. Although he'd never explained why, I always assumed it was something to fill the hole of her absence. To the best of my knowledge, he'd never really looked at another woman after she died. Whatever need and loss he felt was deeply sublimated by spending his weekends with his head underneath the bonnets of old Fords and Holdens.

We all followed him out to the shed to look at the latest project car. An old Kingswood stood in a state of disrepair in the centre of the shed. It looked to me, from a purely practical level, that the thing was too far gone and more trouble than it was worth to get it back into running order. But that wasn't really the point of the exercise for Dad.

He spent an hour or two showing us all the things he was doing or planning to do to the car. A lot of it went over my head but I noticed Courtney nodding and saying "cool" every so often and Paul nodded his interest as well. I felt the warm glow of family again, the warm glow I'd missed when I was trying to make a life in Adelaide and chasing big money on mine sites in

WA. The warm glow that lets you know that here is where you really belong.

After a while Dad and Paul were keen to go to the pub. The SANFL Finals were on and they wanted to watch it on the big screen at the pub with all of Dad's mates. We trudged down the tiny main street of Spalding to the only pub in town.

The game was just about to start when we got there and the pub was pretty full. A local lad, Dad knew him and his family, had shown promise with the local footy team and been recruited to play for North Adelaide in the SANFL. He was playing today; North Adelaide were taking on Glenelg in the preliminary final. All the footy fans in Spalding, and that was nearly everyone, were here to watch and cheer him on. A local making it into the big leagues is always an event for a country town the size of Spalding.

I wasn't yet ready to start drinking properly so I got myself a Coke and hung out with Dad as he caught up with his mates and discussed the game. Courtney wanted to play pool so I joined her at the pool table and we started a game. She had tied her hair up by this point and I couldn't help but think how it made her look so much more like our side of the family. I noticed how aside from the crow-coloured hair she'd inherited from her Kiwi mother, she was well and truly a Mollenberg, one of us all the way through. While she was lining up a shot on the pool table I glanced across at Paul and Dad over towards the bar. Their faces were so similar it was scary. If you added my face to the line up it would have looked like a row of those Easter Island statues, all alike with only superficial differences.

Courtney beat me at pool and started skiting about it to her dad so obviously I had to play her again until I beat her. It took five games for me to get a win over her. Paul, who by this time had sunk several beers, proclaimed he was going to beat his daughter's arse at pool and was defeated soundly three times in a row. Dad decided he needed to uphold the honour of the males of our family. He beat her once and then refused to play anymore despite her insistence that she could whip his arse if she had another go.

By this time the footy had nearly finished. North Adelaide had put up a good fight but Glenelg were ahead and it was clear they were going to win. The local lad had given it a red hot go and people in the pub were happy, even proud of him. They boldly predicted big things for his future. He might go all the way, they said, he could get signed up with one of the AFL clubs if he kept up his form.

I'd had a few beers and Paul and Dad were both three sheets to the wind by the time the game actually ended. We all had the grog munchies, so we got pub meals all round. Seafood basket for Courtney, mixed grill for Paul and parmis for Dad and me. We ate and drank some more, socialised with the locals. Dad introduced me to a bloke called Charlie who I vaguely remembered from some big family gathering years ago.

'Yeah, he's your cousin. Well, second cousin technically, but same thing. Your Uncle Thomas' boy'

Dad set me right and the connection made sense in my mind despite the beer starting to really affect me.

After a while I really felt under the weather. Too much beer and too much socialising were doing me in. Dad and Paul were being social butterflies at the bar; Courtney had found some local teenagers who'd come to the pub with their parents to hang out with. I watched her chatting to some local boy, a couple years older than her but still basically a kid. I could read the body language and knew there was a vibe there. For a moment I thought about intervening and telling the boy to fuck off on the grounds that Courtney was only thirteen but I decided against it. She wasn't my daughter and anyway, teenagers have to learn these things for themselves.

I started to feel nauseous so I walked outside. To my surprise it was dark. I didn't realise it had got so late. We'd blown the whole afternoon watching the footy and drinking and now the stars were out. The air was cold but fresh and clean the way winter air in the country always is. You could smell a few wood fires burning in people's house, hear the occasional truck on the road out of town.

I walked a few metres away from the pub to clear my head and try and get my queasy guts under control. I stopped when I was about thirty metres or so away from the pub and looked back at it. The lights were on and I could hear a little bit of noise. It looked homely and warm, like a beloved home a soldier returns to after the war.

A wave of warmth and love swept over me. I felt sorry for the years I'd wasted trying to make it in the city, chasing money in the mines. I knew that there was nothing the world could give me that could compare to this simple warmth of belonging to this family, this tribe of poor white trash in these little country towns. I knew my place was here in these towns with these people, that the path to happiness for me was to settle down in one of these places and have a family and ignore the wider world. I knew that if I followed this path I would die old and happy in a little town and be buried one day in a little country cemetery surrounded by relatives. Unimportant in the eyes of the world but happy and fulfilled in the ways that really count.

As these emotions washed over me and my stomach struggled with the beer and pub food I knew what I had to do. I took out my phone and called Marissa.

'Oh, hi babe, how's the trip going?'

'Good, babe. I need to ask you something.'

'When I get back do you want to get married and start a family?'

There was a silence for a moment.

'Are you for real? Because if you're just dicking around and making a joke, I'll kill you. This is serious stuff, don't play about with it.'

'No, I'm completely serious babe, I've thought about it. My wandering days are over. I'll get a better job, we'll sort something out, but my mind's made up. I want to settle down with you if you'll have me.'

'Oh God, yes, YES! Oh shit, this is really happening!'

'I'll call you back in the morning and we'll start making plans. I love you.'

I hung up and a few seconds later I lost the battle with my guts and spewed beside the power pole. I wiped my face and stared at the stars, happier than I'd been in years.

'You alright there, old mate?'

A young voice, some teenage boy, enquired out of the darkness. I looked and saw Courtney in the arms of the boy she'd been chatting to inside. It seems I'd interrupted their cheeky pash session in the darkness behind someone's Troopy.

'You're a bit weird sometimes, Uncle Jack.' Courtney shook her head and returned to kissing the local boy.

VIVA ADELAIDE!

I can't recall ever making a good choice in my life. It seems to me, as I look back, that I mostly drifted through life and occasionally reacted to things in an ad hoc way. I never planned anything, never thought through the long-term consequences of my choices in any considered, rational way.

Nonetheless I find myself, in my middle age, surprisingly happy.

I grew up in the Modbury area of Adelaide. A nothing suburb in a nothing city. I spent a great deal of my youth just hanging out and dicking around. There was a skate park I used to hang out at with a bunch of my friends and I find that a great deal of my memories revolve around that skate park.

You could say that it was the skate park that led to the first of my poor choices in life.

I managed to bum around until the end of Year 12, more from a desire to avoid getting a job than any interest in school. School ended and I had no clear plan for my life. I had a job stacking shelves at the big Coles nearby but had no further plans or ambitions beyond that.

That first summer of post-school adult life was pretty damn sweet. All my mates and I were working the sort of jobs kids our age worked; supermarkets, fast food, that sort of thing. We had a little money, could legally buy alcohol and no longer had to bother with school. It felt great. It's just a pity it couldn't last forever.

There was a guy, an older guy, who used to hang out at the skate park. His name escapes me now, I think it was either Tom or Tim or something with a T, definitely. He was 30ish which seemed ancient. His hair was starting to recede but he still dressed and acted like a teenager. He'd come down and skate, smoke bongs, drink beer and talk shit at the skate park.

It hit me one day that he'd been just like me but had never moved on.

It also hit me that unless I took some sort of decisive action, I had a very good chance of ending up just like him.

I remember watching him one afternoon drinking cans of West End at the skate park talking about sluts he claimed to have fucked recently and I looked at his receding hairline and realised this guy was a joke. His life was a joke, he'd never matured beyond high school and never would. His life was the sort of cautionary tale people might tell each other at a high school reunion.

I decided I needed to do something drastic in order to avoid ending up like this guy.

I saw an ad for defence force recruitment on TV that night. I told my mum that I wanted to join. She was keen and helped me fill out the form.

The whole process took a while; tests, interviews, more tests, but every time I saw that guy at the skate park I was sure I was doing the right thing.

In the end I was accepted and enlisted in the Army just shy of my nineteenth birthday.

I thought that this was it. I was going to have a career, make something of myself and avoid the dismal fate of being a middle-aged minimum-waged loser hanging out at the skate park.

But life almost never works out the way you think it will.

Basic training was shit and smashed a lot of illusions about the Army. Mum came to my passing out parade and took the photos of me in my handsome parade uniform and slouch hat that now sit mouldering in her old photo albums.

I went to Singleton to do my infantry training course. There I discovered just how much Army life can suck. This was the "four deployments" era when the Australian Army had troops on the ground in Timor, Solomon Islands, Iraq and Afghanistan and had done for almost a decade. All of our instructors, corporals and sergeants, had done at least one deployment and many had done several. They were, almost without exception, utterly psychotic.

For some reason nobody in the Army hierarchy stopped to consider that taking traumatized men fresh from battlefields and placing them in charge of a bunch of teenagers who were still learning how to be soldiers was not such a great idea.

The bullying and abuse seemed random and without reason. Perhaps it had more to do with which instructor was having PTSD flashbacks at any given time than anything us young privates actually did.

I had one, exactly one, moment of almost genuine humanity and decency from our instructors.

A sergeant named Hollis stopped me one day.

'Private Fallon, you're from SA are you?'

'Yes Sergeant, Modbury to be exact'

'Ah, good spot, I'm from Lobethal myself, not many of us in the Army you know, full of fucking Queenslanders and Tasmanians. Have you noticed?'

I had noticed this as early as the first day of basic training. I assumed it had something to do with unemployment rates and demographics.

'Yes, Sergeant, lots of them, I've noticed.'

He shook his head, disgusted by it all.

'Fucking Tasmanians, may as well be New Zealanders, and fucking Queenslanders are the dregs of this country. Bunch of cousin fuckers, the lot of them, can't fucking stand them. Us Croweaters have to stick together.'

With this he nodded and walked off and that was it, the only small moment of human decency and warmth I ever experienced from anyone in the Army and it was based on nothing more than parochial prejudice and the assumption that I shared said prejudice.

I finished the infantry course at Singleton and was posted to a battalion. The life of an infantry solider is not fun, hard work and training with little relief other than piss-ups on days off and trips to the brothel in town. I'd been better off as a shelf stacker at Coles. I think everyone who joins the military eventually has that moment, when they realise they have made a mistake and the whole thing is bullshit but they still have years to serve on their contract and can't get out of it.

I never drank so much in my life as I did in the Army.

Eventually the battalion I was in got notice that we were going to Afghanistan. Training shifted up a gear, we got ourselves ready. For the history minded folk reading this, we were the second or third last battalion of the Australian Army to do a tour of Afghanistan before the government called time on our commitment there. What that meant was that everyone had well and truly lost enthusiasm for this shit. Nobody believed all that 9/11 bullshit about fighting for freedom and protecting our country. Nobody really believed we were winning anymore. The deployment was something we had to do because someone higher up the chain of command said we had to do it.

A lot of the officers and NCOs had already been once and some had been twice. They knew what we were in for and you could tell they didn't really want to go but they were so accustomed to obeying orders like a robot that it never occurred to them to say "Fuck this shit!" and revolt. They hated it but they did it, like good little slaves.

When we finally got there, when the door of the plane opened and we walked out into the baking heat of Afghanistan, it really hit me. I would've given anything at that moment to be back stacking shelves at Coles. I wanted to apologise to that guy at the skate park, I wanted to tell him I was sorry for thinking him a loser and admit that he was smarter than me. He was probably down the skate park right now, smoking bongs and talking utter shit without a care in the world and here I was, about to be a combatant in a pointless bullshit war in a country that can only be described as the arsehole of the world.

The six months of my deployment were utterly awful. Humping pack and rifle through a country that was stuck in the Bronze Age. Walking over ground that was full of old land-mines and IEDs. Small, shitty, indecisive contacts with an enemy who knew they didn't have to beat us in an open fight but merely keep up a steady stream of corpses home and eventually our government would cut its losses and leave. All of this with the knowledge that nobody back home cared or even really knew what was going on.

The deployment ended and we came home. I was happy I was alive and in one piece. I was furious that I'd wasted six months of my life on this bullshit. I was depressed that I still had just over a year to go on my contract before I could leave the Army.

I managed to bide my time and stay out of trouble for the last year in the Army. About a month before my contract expired I got called into the CO's office.

'Private Fallon, you have less than a month to go on your contract. Your conduct as a soldier has been satisfactory and we would like to offer you promotion to Lance Corporal. You'd have to sign on for another three years and we'd send you on a course but this would mean leadership responsibilities and it would be a significant step forward in your Army career. Are you keen?'

I couldn't help myself. I laughed in his face.

His visage darkened. I knew then I'd fucked up but I didn't care. I was sick of the Army; I despised it and everything it stood for and I didn't care if the battalion CO knew it. If anything, I *wanted* him to know it. I was powerless against the institutional might of the Army and laughing in his face was the only way I could express myself. My David against the Army's Goliath.

Of course, I paid the price for my disrespect. The Army doesn't allow a private to get away with laughing in the face of a full Colonel. I got put on punishment duty for the entirety of my last month in the Army. The Regimental Sergeant Major followed me around and did his best to make my life miserable.

I bore it pretty well. I knew I was almost out and there was only so much they could do to me. On my last day, after I'd filled out the paperwork, handed back my uniform and kit and was in civilian clothes walking to the barracks gate I gave the middle finger salute towards the CO's office and spat on the ground. I have no idea if anybody saw or cared but it felt good.

I went back to my mum's house first up. It took a little while to get the Army out of my system. I reveled in my freedom for the first week or so. I went and did all the "civilian" things I missed while I was in the Army, bumming around the shops, going to the cinema, eating out all the time.

The kids I used to hang around with hadn't changed much. That was the problem. I couldn't relate to them anymore. They'd continued working dead end jobs and bumming around. I'd been a solider and been to Afghanistan. What the fuck did we have to talk about now?

I went to the skate park and saw old mate still there, still talking shit and smoking bongs, still refusing to grow up. His hairline had receded even further and there was a streak or two of grey but essentially he was the same loser I'd seen four years ago. He was timeless.

I stood there looking at him doing the same shit he'd been doing all these years and wondered if I was actually the smart one or not. What had I gained by joining the Army? I got an Afghanistan campaign medal which I would never wear again and a dicky back from humping a pack and rifle. Meanwhile, he'd cruised through life, drinking beer and hanging out at the skate park. I sure didn't feel like I was winning.

I needed a job. The skills I'd learned as an infantry soldier in the Army were useless in the civilian world. This was another big disillusionment. I'd left the Army thinking my experience mattered. I thought my status as an Afghanistan veteran mattered. Did it fuck.

Nobody gave a shit.

The civilian world had continued on its merry way through the decade or more that Australian troops had been in Afghanistan. They barely noticed and cared even less. All those millions of people focused on the great Australian dreams of accumulating wealth and cramming as much pleasure into life as possible. Any number of wars could rage overseas and the people of this country wouldn't care so long as the economy kept ticking along, the sun kept shining and there was beer and sport on the weekends.

In the end, for lack of better options, I got my security license and started working as a security guard. The company I worked for had the contracts for several of the larger shopping centres around Adelaide as well as a couple of hospitals so I was kept busy enough.

The shopping centre work was mostly about stopping shoplifters and preventing junkies from shooting up in the toilets. It had the occasional moment of excitement but was fairly routine.

The hospital work was a lot more interesting. There is always something going on at a large metropolitan hospital. People in one section are leaving this world while people in another section are entering it. Some people having the happiest moment of their lives, welcoming their children into the world, while less than a hundred metres away people are having the worst moment of their lives, identifying the bodies of loved ones. I've often thought that working as a security guard or orderly in a hospital should be mandatory for all aspiring writers and dramatists. You get the full spectrum of the human condition on the one site all laid out in front of you.

The night shifts were the best. There is something about a hospital at night that just feels more real than normal life. In a strange sort of way I thrived on it, the slightly sleazy junkie energy of the place in the hours past midnight worked for me, kept me awake and alive.

Mostly I worked at the Queen Elizabeth Hospital and between their emergency department and their psych ward I was kept busy enough.

I remember one night having to restrain a young guy, he would have been twenty or so, who had been admitted to the psych ward after having an amphetamine psychosis episode. He freaked out right in the admissions part of the psych ward and we all had to hold him down so the doctors could dose him up with heavy duty meds to calm him down and make him manageable.

As the drama ended and he was bundled off to the secure part of the psych ward, nicely sedated, we realised his father was standing there, mouth wide open with shock, watching the whole thing. He didn't say anything, just quietly turned around and walked out, but I felt really awkward about it. After I wrote up my incident report sheet about it, I went to try and find him.

He was standing outside in the car park. I could see he had been crying a bit.

'Sorry you had to see that, old mate. You do realise nobody is trying to hurt your son, right? We just have to restrain patients sometimes to prevent them hurting themselves or staff. Everyone is just trying to help your son get well. He'll be safer in here and he'll get help.'

He didn't say anything at first and I wondered if he had heard me. Eventually he spoke, calmly and quietly, as though he was reciting scripture in church.

'It's very kind of you to say that but I don't really believe it. Oh, I know you're not trying to hurt him, I know you're just doing your job. What I mean is, I don't believe he's going to be helped by all this. This is the third time he's been admitted to this place and each time he goes back out there and does more drugs then ever. I put him in rehab and he quit halfway through the program and went and did drugs. I've taken him to Narcotics Anonymous meetings, I've taken him to church, I've taken him to psychiatrists; nothing has worked. I have begun to accept the idea that my son is going to keep doing drugs until he's dead or brain damaged which amounts to the same thing in my book.'

He stopped and watched a car pull out of the carpark and drive off.

'I have to accept that the last twenty years of my life have been futile. I did everything I could for my son. I worked for him, I spent as much time as I could with him, I agonized over his health and education, I went without things so that he could go to a private school and get a better education and have more options in life and now I know for almost certain that he's going to die in the gutter, an addict and a waste of life, and there is nothing I can do about it.'

'So what was the point? Why did I bother? What do I do now that I know it was all for nothing? Now that I know I've failed at the only thing that really matters in life? What do I do now? What do I do?'

I saw tears form and, to my shame, I decided this was beyond my pay grade. I retreated back inside and found something to keep myself occupied for a few hours until I could be reasonably sure the old man had wandered off.

It was about this time my back troubles started to give me real grief.

Roman Legionnaires used to refer to themselves as the Emperor's mules because of the heavy burdens they had to carry on their backs. Any modern infantry soldier can tell you that nothing has changed in two thousand years. The life of an infantry soldier is one of aching feet and crippling back pain.

I'd done my share of humping a pack and it had done me no good. Add to that being on my feet all the time as a security guard as well as getting slightly older and probably not living a really healthy life and I started to really feel it.

I went and saw the doctor. I had a card from the Department of Veterans' Affairs which I thought might mean I got better help. How wrong I was. As soon as the doctor saw it his eyes lit up like a thief seeing the keys have been left in the ignition of a car.

Apparently, there was some sort of subsidy/funding arrangement involving the pharmaceutical companies and the DVA. The end result was that by producing my DVA card, I could get prescriptions for all manner of painkillers dirt cheap and without anyone asking questions.

I found myself fairly quickly using them in a way that wasn't exactly the prescribed manner.

I discovered the warm and pleasant opiate stone and wondered where it had been all my life. At first it was mild enough; take a few more than prescribed and lay on the couch listening to music in a lovely warm funk. Then I started taking just one to get through long cold nights at work. Then I started getting good and properly stoned on my days off and vegetating the whole day away.

Then I crashed my car under the influence and lost my driver's license and my job.

None of this stopped me. The doctors were more than happy to keep prescribing me this shit so long as I waved my little card from the Department of Veterans' Affairs. I was a subsidized, legalized, government-approved junkie.

Without a job and a car I had trouble keeping up with the rent. I gave up my flat and moved into a room upstairs at the old Squatter's Arms pub. I knew one of the bartenders from when he'd been an orderly at the hospital. He also lived in a room upstairs and told me he was only doing it temporarily to save money while he worked on his music career. I didn't care, it was cheap and nobody bothered me; I could get my prescription and vegetate the rest of the day away without being hassled. The pub owner didn't care so long as I paid the minimal rent every week and didn't create drama.

I barely went outside for twelve months. Trips to the doctor for more scripts, getting those scripts filled at the chemist. I maybe ate once a day, usually just some food hall Chinese or something similar if I was in the city, and sometimes I missed a day. Food isn't a priority when you're an addict.

My mum grew very concerned and began to hassle me. I had enough sense through the opiate fog to realise this wasn't a lifestyle I could continue. I began to look for options.

At first, I went to the Department of Veterans' Affairs office and asked them. They told me to fill out forms and directed me to websites but weren't much help.

My mum found this place, a rehab run by the Salvation Army. They were willing to take me, a week to detox then seven weeks of program. I remember my last night living in the little room above the pub. I couldn't sleep and I had taken the last of my pills. I spent hours just staring out the grimy window of my little room at the traffic on Port Road. The sun began to rise, the traffic intensified, I got a message from my mum asking if I was ready to go. I got up and headed downstairs feeling unwell and fragile. A new and hopefully better phase of my life was about to begin.

Detoxing from a serious opiates habit is one of the least fun things you can ever do. I felt like I was dying for at least four days before it levelled out and I just felt godawful for another three days or so.

I met her on the fifth day of detox.

I was in the little yard of the detox section that resembled a cage and was used by the patients as a smoking and pacing area. People in varying states of unwellness would come out here for a little smoke and pace around trying to exorcise whatever demons they were bothered by.

I found a small sunny patch and sat, face towards the sun, its healing rays baking my aching body.

She sat down less than a metre away from me.

'Sun good today?' she asked casually.

'Feels alright but I'm not exactly healthy enough to properly appreciate it.'

'Oh contraire, when you're unwell is exactly when you can really appreciate simple, natural pleasures like sitting in the sun.'

I turned and looked at her. She wore all black and it matched her jet black hair. She looked like a sadder, gothier version of Eva Green at a glance. She was tall, lanky, a real beanpole girl and the way she sat on the ground dressed in all black she resembled a spider making itself comfortable in a corner of a web. She was wafer thin but so was I, the ravages of addiction make everyone thin, sometimes dangerously so. I never saw a single fat person during my time in rehab.

You could tell she was fragile, just holding it together, but there was an edge of defiance to her, a will to live that had apparently kept her alive through her addiction and was now burning a little bit brighter here in detox.

She clocked me looking at her and turned her face away from the sun to look at me.

'So, what are you in for?' A strand of that jet black hair fell over her face.

'Getting off a pile of prescription opiates, not much fun. How about you?'

'Heroin, three-year habit, bitch of a thing. Not that I ever plan on doing the shit again but how did you get enough prescription opiates to get a habit? I thought they were pretty tight on that shit?'

'Afghanistan veteran, I have a little card from the Department of Veterans' Affairs, it works wonders, like a magic wand to doctors.'

'Ah, I see …'

We sat in silence for a little bit, faces turned back towards the sun, the baking warmth making us feel just that little bit alive.

'So what's your plan?'

'My plan?'

'For what comes after this. It's one thing to detox off the shit, it's another to start living again clean. Do you have any idea what you're going to do?'

I didn't really have anything thought out.

'Dunno, just live I suppose, find some way to move forward in life. Get my driver's license back, get a job or something. Something along those lines.'

She nodded sagely.

'Planning on staying clean or getting back into the fray?'

The question seemed cynical and awful to me.

'Of course I plan on staying clean, what's the fucking point of being here if you don't? Why put myself through detox if I'm just going back on the shit?'

She smiled a warm, kind smile.

'I wasn't accusing you of anything, but not everyone in here is sincere. See her over there?'

I looked at the middle-aged woman in surprisingly nice clothes pacing back and forth in one corner of the yard.

'Her name is Belinda Hamilton, she's from an old money eastern suburbs family, I went to school with her niece. She's a raging alcoholic who thinks she can't possibly be an alcoholic because she comes from a nice family and has loads of money. This is her second or third trip to rehab. She stays sober for a little while, like nine months or so at a time then gets back on the piss. Thinks she's so much better than the rest of us because of her family and her money. I can't stand the bitch. She hates me too, she knows that I know who she is because I went to school with her niece. She thinks I'm going to spread the story of her disgrace all around the social circles of Burnside.'

'Will you? Spread the story I mean.'

She sighed and shook her head gently before replying.

'I try and avoid my family and their bullshit social circle as much as possible. Although I have to admit it is tempting to air this bitch's dirty laundry at certain dinner parties my parents go to. I'm sure she makes up elaborate lies about where she is right now. A holiday in Greece is much more socially acceptable than a trip to rehab, if you know what I mean.'

'What would happen if you did let the cat out of the bag?'

She laughed a bitter laugh before turning her face back towards the sun.

'Everyone would pretend they didn't know anything to her face but they'd be talking about it non-stop for weeks. She'd know of course and it would eat her up inside. These people live and die on the opinions of their peers.'

I thought about what she'd told me for a few minutes and enjoyed the sun a little more until it occurred to me to ask another question.

'So, if you went to school with her niece, I take it you're from that part of town as well?'

She smiled again and I couldn't help thinking how lovely she looked with her jet black hair and her small but sincere smile.

'Oh yeah, I am a genuine Burnside trust fund princess, blue blood and an expensive education, the whole deal. Bet you've never met one before, have you?'

'Can't say I have, no.'

'Where did you grow up then?'

'Modbury.'

'You say that like it's a prison sentence, "Modbury", just a lump of a word. Surely it's not that bad, is it?'

'Well, when I was nineteen I joined the Army because it seemed a better option than staying in Modbury. Does that answer your question?'

She laughed a little.

'You know, I don't think anyone from my old school joined the Army. They all seem to become doctors, lawyers, investment bankers and that sort of thing.'

'And junkies?'

'Oh, that's just me, I'm a disgrace to the proud name of Burnside and Walford girls school.'

She smiled a jolly, life affirming smile at me as she said this and I think I fell in love with her then. There is really something in being able to find humour in your own misfortune and poor life choices, it really says something about your character.

'But seriously there are more of us than you might think, we just tend to be better at hiding it and we can afford interstate rehabs where we have less chance of being seen by anyone we know. My parents wanted me to go to a rehab in Sydney for that exact reason. I refused because fuck them and their precious family name. I'll own my poor life choices and I'll recover from them on my own terms.'

She seemed determined as she said this and I felt quite strongly that here was an admirable woman. I wanted to keep talking but we were called inside for a group session at that time.

Rehab was a routine of group sessions, one on one counselling and being taken in the van to Narcotics Anonymous meetings. I liked it as much as it's possible to like such things. I liked the camaraderie of the NA meetings, the feeling that we're all fuck ups united in the desire to try again and have another crack at life. That felt good. Much better than slogging it out alone. Mostly I just liked the idea that I was coming to life again. That the grim times were over and there was hope on the horizon. That felt good. Really good.

In between all this I often sat in that same sunny patch of the yard at the rehab. Sasha often sat with me and we had little conversations about various things.

'I've been meaning to ask you about your name,' she said out of the blue one day in that first week.

'My name?'

'Yeah, when you shared at the meeting last night you said your name was Charlie.'

'Yeah, it is.'

'On your birth certificate?'

'Ah, no, that reads Charles but everyone calls me Charlie and always has done.'

'Thought so.'

'What about you? Is Sasha short for anything? Or is it a fake name to hide your true identity?'

She laughed. 'No, it's my real name, but you'll find I don't let my family name be known if I can help it. When people realise who I'm related to their behavior sometimes changes.'

'What's your family name?'

She told me. I knew who she was related to immediately. Adelaide is not that big and the big money families who own stuff and run the political scene are well known. No wonder she tried to keep a lid on it.

'You're not going to be weird about it, are you?'

'No, doesn't make any difference to me.'

'Good, you're a good sort, Charlie.'

It felt like a connection was being made.

Rehab ended after seven weeks. I found a place to live that was cheap. It was a house on Churchill Road just a couple of hundred metres south of the Reepham Hotel. It was one of the older houses that had survived the waves of gentrification and development that had engulfed the area. The owner was renting it out as student accommodation. I told her some bullshit story about planning to study soon but honestly, I don't think she cared that much. She told me how much, I paid, she gave me a key, that was about it.

The room was fairly basic, it had a bed and a wardrobe. Most importantly it had a lock on the door so I had that little bit of extra privacy. The other tenants in the other rooms were all Taiwanese students. They barely spoke English but they were quiet and clean and didn't bother me. They would sit in the lounge room watching movies on some Chinese language streaming service I'd never heard of. They'd see me sit down with a cup of tea and press a button that put English language subtitles on whatever they were watching. I thanked them politely every time they did this although I had no real interest in the movies they watched.

My life was fairly desolate to start off with. Coming off the drugs and going through rehab doesn't automatically make your life wonderful. I had no job, the dole money I got was just enough to pay rent and feed myself, my only social interaction was NA meetings. I walked up to the Prospect Library after living in the house for a week and got myself a library card. That was all the entertainment I could afford.

I was still without a driver's license and would be for a little while longer so I had to use public transport to get to meetings.

I remember taking the bus into the city one afternoon and wondering where exactly I was going in life. I had to switch buses in the city to catch one down to Unley where there was an NA meeting at the Salvo hall. As my second bus pulled out of the city and traversed the green of the south parklands, I had a small moment of quiet despair. How the fuck had I ended up a broke, unemployed, recovering addict using public transport in my thirties?

Although I had stopped diving headfirst into failure by getting clean it was painfully obvious to me that I still wasn't really winning in life. Add to that this cold, raw emptiness that seemed to hollow me out ever since getting clean and losing the warm oblivion of opiates. It was like losing a limb but you got less sympathy.

By the time the bus got to Unley and I got off I was feeling like cold dogshit in the rain.

The guy who ran this meeting, a toothless former meth addict from Hackam West known to everyone as Jeep, was just setting up as I arrived. For lack of anything better to do I gave him a hand setting out chairs. When we had it more or less organised he made us both a cup of cheap-shit coffee and we sat down while waiting for people to arrive.

'You're what? Two months clean now? How's it going? Still a struggle?'

'Shit yeah, not like feeling tempted to use again or anything like that. It's just life is so fucking grey and empty now, and I still don't feel like I'm getting anywhere or doing anything even approaching successful. It's like my life is just treading water. When does anything good happen?'

He laughed a small bitter laugh.

'Why would anything good happen? This is Adelaide!'

Amused by his own wit he laughed a little more before becoming serious and continuing the conversation.

'Listen, let me tell you something. I'm four years clean, four and a half actually, and life has only just started getting good. Don't expect a miracle in your first few months. Actually, you're already living the miracle, you're clean. Don't ever lose sight of that. Every day clean is a victory.'

He sipped his shitty coffee before continuing.

'You've got to remember that your body is going through a whole massive chemical change, a full fucking reset. Can't expect that to be over and done and everything back to normal in a few months. Case in point, your little habit there.'

He pointed at the bag of lollies I was dipping into as we talked.

'What?'

'You've been hitting that shit pretty hard since you got clean, haven't you?'

'Yeah, how'd you know?' I asked as I chewed.

'Everyone does it, it's your dopamines.'

'My dopamines?'

'Yeah, like the addiction and pleasure chemicals in your brain. They've been getting big hits from drugs for years, now you're clean, your brain is looking for a substitute. Happens to everyone who gets clean, we all eat mountains of sugary shit and put on weight but hey, if it helps you stay clean, go for it. What're you on, anyway?'

I showed him the packet like a naughty child caught dipping his hand into the cookie jar.

'Spearmint leaves, I'm on them all the time. They're like crack to me since I got clean.'

Jeep chuckled, happy to have his pseudo-scientific theory validated.

'Yep, it's your dopamines.'

Other people started arriving for the meeting.

Sasha walked in and I was happy to see her again. After the meeting we walked outside together.

'So where're you living now?' she asked as we stood just outside the door of the Salvos Hall.

'Churchill Road, just down from the Reepham pub, living with a bunch of Taiwanese students. It's basic but it'll do for now. How about you?'

'I'm up in Cheltenham not far from the old cemetery. I'm living with Tanya and Debbie, they're both in recovery as well so it kind of works out well. I take it you're still clean, then?'

'Yeah, and you?'

'Yeah, bit of a struggle some days but sticking with it. What are you doing with yourself now?'

I shrugged. I had no money and no plans. 'Catching the bus home, I suppose.'

'Well, I'll catch the bus into the city with you and then I'm catching the train to Cheltenham. C'mon.'

We talked as we waited for the bus and continued talking as the bus took us into the city. For the first time in two months I felt good and alive again. The lights of the city, the beautiful smile of Sasha as she sat with me and talked. It was almost enough to make me forget that I was a washed-up veteran and recovering addict in his thirties.

We parted company on North Terrace; she had a train to catch and I had a northbound bus to catch. We promised to see each other again at another meeting. As my bus took me up Churchill Road, I felt something warm and hopeful stirring in my chest. I finished my pack of spearmint leaves sitting on the bus.

The Taiwanese students were all out doing whatever it was that Taiwanese students did on a Saturday night. The house was deathly silent, only the gentle hum of traffic from Churchill

Road could be heard. I was hungry so I went through my shelf in the kitchen cupboard looking for something to eat. It was a depressing enterprise. I was poor and ate poor as a result; tinned shit and pasta in the cupboard, eggs and plain brand cheese in the fridge, the taste of poverty. For lack of better options I cracked open a tin of Tom Piper Savoury Mince and Vegetables, cooked it up and put it on some toast.

I sat at the table and put the TV on for some background noise. The Taiwanese students only ever watched their Chinese language streaming service; I had no money for a streaming service so it was free-to-air TV for me. Unwatchable shitty reality shows or old movies I'd already seen years ago. *Jumanji* was on. I sat down and looked at the tinned food I'd heated up for dinner. I looked at the empty house and felt a cold loneliness that even a Robin Williams movie couldn't heal.

'Fuck my life.' I muttered to myself and began to eat my savoury mince and vegetables on toast.

One week went on after another, becoming a month and then two and then three. I stayed clean and so did Sasha. We became firm friends and spent a fair bit of time together. I was poverty stricken but she was still a trust fund princess and with the drain of financing a heroin habit gone her trust fund stretched quite a ways. She understood how broke I was and would sometimes shout us both lunch after a meeting, nothing fancy. If we were near the city we'd go to the Chinatown food hall off Grote Street. It's amazing how much of a morale boost a simple feed of food hall Chinese and a chat with a friend can be.

'I'm thinking I need to get a job,' I said one day.

'Ok, any particular reason for that?'

'I'm sick to fuck of being broke for starters. Also, I need more out of life than what I've got right now. Literally, all I do is go to meetings, hang out with you and go to the Prospect library. I'm going to run out of books to read soon, I reckon I've read a fair chunk of what the library has. I need to broaden my horizons a bit.'

'Don't regret or apologise for being well read, it makes you more interesting and intelligent than 90% of the population. But seriously, you think a job is what you need?'

'It would get me out and about and put a bit more money in my pocket and that's plenty right now.'

'So what job are you planning to get then?'

'Well, there lies the problem. I don't have a car or license, it's a few more months before I can get my license back and even then I don't have money for a car. I also have a shit resumé: teenage shelf stacker at Coles, soldier, security guard, on the dole for a couple years. That's it. Doesn't give me hope.'

Neither of us had a solution for this problem at the time. I thought about it for a week and when I saw Jeep again at the Unley meeting I told him about it. He offered a solution straight up.

'Go for the fast food places, they hire any cunt.'

'For real?'

'Yeah, that's what I did when I first got clean; worked at the Macca's across from the horse races at Morphetville. Did that for … shit it must have been nearly two years. Started doing TAFE part time the second year I worked there, got my certificate and got a better job and there you go.'

'So they aren't bothered about hiring addicts in recovery?'

'Shit mate, half the cunts you see in meetings work or have worked for them. It's like one of those symbolic relationships between recovering addicts with shit resumés and fast food joints that nobody wants to work at.'

'You mean a symbiotic relationship?'

'Yeah, like them clown fish and enemies.'

'You mean anemones?'

'Yeah them *Finding Nemo* cunts'

He sipped his cuppa and gathered himself to fully explain it all to me.

'You see, no cunt wants to work in fast food. I mean, teenagers do it after school and that but nobody aspires to it, do they? So they can't get bodies half the time and the people they do get don't want to be there any longer than they have to. You look at any given fast food joint and over half the adult staff are putting out resumés and applications to better jobs while they're working there. So what they want is people who will stay for longer periods of time. In comes us addicts in recovery, we've all got highly dubious resumés and that's putting it politely. No decent job is going to have us. But fast food joints will. In fact, I know for a fact they actually look for us. You got a key tag?'

I did. NA groups gave out little plastic key tags for clean time. I'd recently got my three months clean tag.

'Right, apply and when you go for an interview, casually as you can, hold your keys in your hand and let the tag be visible. They'll snap you up because they know you can't get anything better and are more likely to stay a long time. I'm telling you, it's a relationship.'

'So other people in recovery do these jobs?' I didn't want to be the only loser working a deep fryer.

'Yeah, old mate Terry, you know him, he works at the Hungry Jack's in Port Adelaide. Bella, you know Bella, she works at the Macca's on West Terrace there. Steve was working at the KFC in Glenelg but he's moved on to greener pastures now. Plenty of people in recovery do it as a first job once they're clean.'

It made sense and I thought about it during the meeting. Afterwards, when I caught the bus home with Sasha, I told her what Jeep had said.

'Makes sense, I suppose. I wonder if it is really as widespread as he says? How many cheeseburgers have I eaten that were cooked by recovering addicts?'

I got home that night and after a dismal dinner of beans on toast I decided I had nothing to lose by applying. I went online and filled out the form, attached my pitiful excuse of a resumé, and sent it in.

I got asked to come in for an interview within a day.

It was the KFC in Prospect there on Main North Road. Walking distance from where I was living and the first to reply. It would do, I decided, as I walked in to do the interview. If they offer me the job, I'm taking it.

I needn't have worried.

The interview lasted all of five minutes. The manager was a young woman named Cate who looked young to me, although she must have been in her early twenties. I took Jeep's tip and casually fondled my keys letting my key tag be seen. I don't know if it made any difference, I think she had already made up her mind to hire me before I even showed up. A few bullshit questions to which I gave bullshit answers and voila! I was hired.

I was leaving the ranks of the disreputable unemployed and joining the fraternity of productive citizens. It almost felt like something good and meaningful.

There was a pile of paperwork and hours of corporate videos to watch for training but once things got underway properly, it wasn't too bad. I had asked specifically not to be out front serving customers. I couldn't bear being nice to random fuckwits all day; I asked to be behind the scenes in the kitchen and they were fine with that.

I met a friend in that kitchen who is still a friend to this day.

His name was Trevor, an older guy who looked like life had really given him a beating. His face looked like it was carved in stone, utterly without joy or even a small spark of human warmth. His expression never changed: the perfect image of grim unhappiness.

It was strange to see the teenagers out front full of life and smiling and then in the kitchen out of public view there was old Trevor and myself, old blokes battered by life and not exactly winning or happy.

My first shift I worked out Trevor's' deal. When we packed up and were about to leave he got his keys out of his pocket and I saw his keyring with the Alcoholics Anonymous symbol on it. There was no one else in the staff room so I took a punt.

'You're a friend of Bill Wilson's?' I said gesturing to his keyring. His facial expression never changed.

'Yeah, and you?'

'Yeah, I'm in the other lot, NA.'

He nodded and said nothing further at the time but I must have been deemed alright in his book because the day after when we worked together again he invited me to lump in with him.

'Here, chuck yours in with mine and we'll have a proper bucket.' He had got an empty go-bucket from out front and put it on the shelf above the breading table where he was working. He filled it with his lollies, Black Cats, and invited me to put my Spearmint Leaves in with them. It seemed rude not to so I chucked mine in with his. I was privately pleased to find out that Jeep's theory about dopamine was apparently correct and universal.

As if reading my thoughts he offered his commentary as I poured my lollies into the bucket.

'Happens to every alco and addict in recovery, mate. We all get hooked on this shit instead of our old habits. Dopamines and all that you know, got to watch them dopamines.'

With that deeply scientific advice our friendship and working together began.

I learnt how to use the deep fryers and clean and avoid contaminating anything but above all else how to be fast on my feet and keep the pace required. A suburban KFC operates at a fair old clip and is rarely not busy. Being in that kitchen got me back to doing things with a sense of urgency again after years of idle nothingness.

Trevor and I formed a little tag team of grumpy old bastards who were separate, in a way, from the teenagers and young adults out front. We were older men who'd experienced hard times in life and knew what failure, loneliness and poverty were. The kids out front still had the unbridled optimism of youth.

In between bursts of activity and handfuls of lollies, we'd sometimes have little chats.

'How long you been in recovery? How long you been clean?' Trevor asked me early on.

'About four and a half months now, almost five. Went through the Salvos rehab.'

'Good stuff, stick with it mate, life does get better.' As he said this his cold stone visage never altered even in the slightest. It would have been almost impossible for anyone to tell he was actually being encouraging and supportive just by looking at him.

Just then Cate, the young female manager who'd hired me, came out back and vivaciously announced sales figures.

'Hey guys! Just letting you know that we've hit our top sales figures for the month so well done team! Very proud of everyone, give yourselves a pat on the back!'

She said it so sincerely and with so much enthusiasm that you were forced to the horrifying realization that she actually meant it. She sincerely cared about this dead end minimum wage job and believed in it.

Trevor and I stared at her for a second before Trevor spoke.

'I once drank metho for so long I had a fit, shat blood and nearly died and it was less painful than listening to that bullshit.'

His face was unchanged as he said this. The cold, immortal stone of a Pharoah's death mask.

Cate thought he was joking.

'Oh Trevor, we love you, we really do, the store comedian, always making jokes!'

She flitted back to the front of the store and out of our hair. Trevor waited until she'd gone then made a point to me.

'Make a note of this, mate. Being clean and sober and doing recovery is the best thing you'll ever do in your life, but, and this is an important but, the rest of the world doesn't understand or care. They won't give you a big reward for it and they expect you to get with their program and participate in their bullshit. You survive horrors and years of degradation and get on the program and then find yourself taking orders from a spastic trollop like her. Such is life.'

'So how'd you end up working here, Trevor?'

'My resumé was shit, twenty years of active alcoholism, couple of stints in jail, couple of years sleeping in the parklands, but this lot hire any cunt.'

With that we got back to work.

I got the hang of the job. I got used to being employed again. I had something to fill my days for the first time in years. Even better, I actually had a little money.

I insisted Sasha let me buy us both lunch one day to make up for all the food hall Chinese she'd shouted me.

'So KFC is working out for you?'

'Yeah, I mean it's a shit job really but it's a job, I'm off the dole and making a little money and I have a reason to get up every morning. I know it's kind of pathetic but I feel like I'm getting somewhere.'

'Small progress is still progress.'

'Apparently so. How about you? What's happening in your life?'

She sighed before she spoke and I could tell there was some struggle going on.

'Where to start? Being clean again means my family are on speaking terms with me again and this is not actually a good thing. Honestly, if you met my family you'd be like "that's why she did heroin" they are just that toxic. But now I'm in recovery I'm apparently obliged to have some sort of active relationship with them. It's exhausting and demoralizing.'

She sighed again before continuing.

'Add to that I'm like eighty percent sure my housemates are using again so isn't that just a shit in your pudding?'

'Tanya and Debbie are on the gear again? Are you sure?'

'Mostly sure, you know, all the little lies and dishonesties that addicts practice when they're using? Not coming out of their rooms for days and then having elaborate explanations ready when I casually ask them where they've been and what they've been doing. They've both stopped bothering with meetings and the matches we kept in the kitchen to light the

160

stove keep disappearing as do the spoons in the drawers. You add it all up and tell me what you think is going on.'

I nodded my head. There was no denying it looked as bad as she said. We both knew the signs and what they meant.

'So what are you going to do?'

'Well, it's not my name on the lease so if they are I'll just bail and get the fuck out of there. I'm not putting my recovery at risk. If they want to use they can do it without me around.'

She stopped and looked me directly in the eyes before speaking again.

'Charlie, can I ask a favor? If I have to get out in a hurry and don't have a new place lined up for a little while, is it alright if I crash with you? Just temporarily.'

Without stopping to think what I was committing myself to I answered.

'Of course mate, I mean, I don't really have much room and you'd have to navigate your way around the Taiwanese students but if it's just temporary, I don't see a problem.'

She thanked me and we talked some more before parting. She gave me a hug, the first time she'd done that, as we left each other. It felt good and as I walked away to catch my bus I thought how fortunate I was to have a friend like her.

I went home full of the first warm happiness I'd felt in years.

Predictably enough Sasha's troubles came to a head a week later.

I had just got home from KFC, long enough to have a shower, get changed and make a cuppa. When I opened the door to her I knew right away what had happened but she insisted, as I sat her down and made her a cup of tea, on telling me every little detail.

'I got home and they were there, Tanya and Debbie, just cooking up on the coffee table in the lounge room like it was no big deal. I was all like "what the fuck are you doing" and Tanya looked me straight in the eyes and said "what does it fucking look like we're doing?"

'I tried reasoning with them, you know, guys what about your recovery? And all that sort of thing. They told me to fuck off with that shit. Said I could either join in or fuck off but they weren't going to listen to my shit.'

'Tanya shot up right in front of me, no fucking shame at all, I saw the shot hit her, saw the heroin bliss hit her brain and her eyes roll back. God, it was beautiful and disgusting at the same time. Like watching someone else have an orgasm.'

'I went to my room and tried to think, Charlie, for like a second, maybe a couple of seconds, I thought about joining in, I really did. God, it's always there, isn't it? That temptation never entirely goes away, does it?'

'Anyway, I just sort of stood there in my room for a couple minutes. I went back and forth in my mind but in the end I packed my shit and got out of there.'

'As I'm walking out Tanya is stoned out of her box on the couch and leans over and grabs my arm. She's completely fuck-eyed and her face looks like the cover of *The Bends*. She grabs me and says "C'mon, join in, don't be a stuck-up cunt." I shook her off and got out of there.'

She paused, almost in tears, obviously feeling the strain of a very emotional day.

'And here I am.'

'And here you are.'

'Is it alright if I crash with you? Just for a little while?' she said, a tremble in her voice.

'Of course, mate, it's not luxury but we'll manage.'

There was an old single mattress stashed in the hallway cupboard. Presumably it had belonged to a previous tenant and nobody had bothered to chuck it out. I set it out for her with a blanket at the foot of my bed and apologised for the basic accommodation.

'Doesn't matter, I'm happy to be clean still, happy to have a friend like you as well, good things like that … you've got to remember how lucky you are sometimes, got to remember to be a little grateful.'

She hugged me then and kissed me affectionately on the cheek and for a moment I felt like I was some sort of noble, heroic person saving society instead of a recovering addict and worn out veteran who worked at KFC and was letting a friend sleep on his floor.

I didn't have to work for a few days so we hung out at home while she settled down and tried to think what she was going to do now. The Taiwanese students accepted her without too much bother. She introduced herself as "Charlie's friend, Sasha" and they took it in their stride. She made me cups of tea while I did my laundry and pottered about the house. She drew the line at eating my tinned shit for dinner and insisted we order something in. Her trust fund meant she never had to endure poverty food the way I did.

We went to a meeting and apparently word had already got around about Tanya and Debbie's falling off the wagon. The other women in recovery fussed over Sasha and asked her if she was alright and did she need someone to talk to? All that sort of thing.

Much more subtly I had a cuppa with Jeep and told him about what had happened.

'Those two were never serious about recovery, if you ask me. Some people just want a breather before they get back into it, never had any intention of staying clean for good. Good on

Sasha for making that choice though, she's alright. So what are you two?'

'What do you mean what are we?'

'Well, you're sleeping together, aren't you? What, if anything, does it mean?'

'We're not!' I protested perhaps a little too much. 'She's sleeping in my bedroom but not in my bed, just on a mattress on the floor temporarily like, when she sorts things out she'll move on.'

Jeep chuckled cynically.

'Sure mate, you believe what you need to believe. But I'll tell you what, when you finally do it your fucking head will get blown off.'

'What? Why?'

'Dopamines,' he said with a confidence that only bro science can produce. 'Your dopamines haven't really been given a proper run since you got clean. First time you fuck after getting clean always blows your head off. You'll see, got to watch them dopamines.'

With this disconcerting prophecy we headed back into the meeting.

A day or two later I was back at work and told Trevor all about what had happened. To my surprise, he sided with Jeep.

'She's sleeping in your bed?'

'No, just in my bedroom, she's got a mattress on the floor.'

'That's only temporary, you two are going to fuck sure as chickens lay eggs. When you do it'll blow your fucking head off.'

'Let me guess, dopamines?'

'Too right, got to watch them dopamines.'

'Is this just one of those old wives' tales that does the rounds in recovery or is there any evidence for this?'

'After I'd been sober for a while, not long after I started here actually, I thought since I had a little money coming in I may as well go get a root and make up for the long years of useless whiskey dick.'

'Please let this be the end of your story, Trevor.'

'… so off I went to the knocking shop. Got a nice girl, all was going well until we got to the funny part and I thought I was dying it was so intense. All them dopamines you see, first time after getting clean and sober is always like that. You'll see.'

He kept the same stone cold grim expression on his face the entire time.

A week or two passed, things settled down and Sasha and I relaxed a little. She didn't seem in a rush to move and to be honest I didn't really want her to leave. She stayed sleeping on the mattress on the floor but never complained or made much effort to find a place of her own. She got on alright with the Taiwanese students and borrowed my library card. I'd come home in the afternoons sometimes and find her on the couch with a book and the radio tuned to Three D. It felt warm and good and as close to happy as I could recall feeling.

We spent every moment I wasn't at work together. We'd either hang out at the house or go to a meeting and once or twice we'd splash out and go to the cinema.

'We should go to the footy this weekend,' I said one Friday after I got home from work.

'The footy? Why?'

'It's the last round before the finals and I haven't been to a game in donkey's years. I used to go quite regular when I was young.'

'What game and where?'

'Central Districts vs Glenelg at Elizabeth Oval. We can get there by train, it's all good, it'll be a nice day out.'

'Oh, you mean the state league?'

'Yeah, the SANFL, Mum used to take me sometimes when I was a kid. I always had a good time.'

'I've literally never been to a game in my life.'

'That's appalling, your citizenship should be revoked, downright un-Australian.'

Saturday morning came and she agreed to come with me, somewhat reluctantly. This was clearly an experience beyond the normal for a Burnside girl.

'You want to wear the beanie or the scarf?' I asked

'Why do I have to wear either of them?'

'Because it's tradition, now pick one!'

She took the beanie as if being handed a dead possum and reluctantly pulled it on her head.

We took the train and had the misfortune to be sitting just across from two plastic gangsta wannabes who were practicing their rapping skills loud enough for us to hear. Pimply white kids wearing tracksuits and expensive sneakers trying to become something like 50 Cent. It was awful.

'Nah bro, drop a beat for me, I've got fresh rhymes, go for it.'

The other one started a half-arsed beatbox sound while his mate warmed up, ready to drop lyrics.

'Got the best weed, got what you need, bitches love me, dogs can suck me, I'm the king of Elizabeth, you can't touch me.'

Sasha had to hide her face in my shoulder to prevent her laughter being heard.

We got off at Elizabeth and walked around to the oval.

The game kicked off and I started to enjoy myself. I could see Sasha was more watching the crowd than the game, the people watching aspect of it more interesting than the actual sport. This being a Central Districts home game, the crowd was a little rough. One woman near us kept going absolutely off her lips at the players as if sheer rage and volume could make them play better.

'STOP FUMBLING THE BALL YOU DOG ROOTING INDIVIDUAL!'

'PUT SOME FUCKING EFFORT IN AND RUN PROPERLY!'

'WHO ARE YOU EVEN KICKING IT TO YOU CLUELESS MUPPET!'

Her exhortations could be heard all over the oval but seemed to have no effect on the home team, who struggled to hold a narrow lead over the visitors.

At half time we wandered over to the food van and got hot dogs. We sat and ate them as grey clouds loomed in from the south.

'So, are you enjoying your first ever footy game?'

'It's fascinating, someone should write a book about it; a truly fascinating cultural phenomenon.'

'Don't do that.'

'Do what?'

'That "I'm too cool for footy" hipster bullshit. It's condescending and fake, just let go of your need to be cool and enjoy things for what they are.'

'I'm not a hipster.'

'Well, when you say things like that you sound like one.'

'Then I'll take your advice and relax and enjoy things.' She reached out and playfully squeezed my hand as she said this and I felt something so intense that I had to look away and pretend to be watching the players coming out again for the third quarter.

About halfway through the third quarter the grey clouds had become black and threatening. Sure enough, with almost no warning the rain hit and hit hard. Sasha and I were on the wrong side of the oval. The sheltered area was over the other side. We ran as the field became a muddy quagmire.

We seemed to get wetter no matter how fast we ran and by the time we made it to the sheltered area we were drenched. We stood there dripping wet. Facing each other, we began to laugh, slightly out of breath but full of life. Sasha's jet black hair was soaked and clung to her like a damp towel as she smiled and laughed. For the first time it really hit me how beautiful she was, how much I cared about her and how much all the struggles we'd been through together meant.

And then she leaned over and kissed me.

As I remember it now I could swear I heard music or saw lights or something. Such a profoundly blissful and meaningful experience like that ought to have a soundtrack I feel.

I don't remember the rest of the game. I cannot, for the life of me, recall if Central Districts held onto their narrow lead and secured a place in the finals or not. I remember taking the train home with Sasha and holding hands with her feeling the gentle rattle of the train. I remember getting home, noting that only one of the Taiwanese students was home and watching a movie in the lounge room. I remember going into my room with Sasha and undressing together for the first time and I remember, true to the predictions of Jeep and Trevor, my head being blown off the first time I had sex since getting clean. Turns out the bro science was accurate after all. Got to watch them dopamines.

We lay together afterwards, getting our breath back and recovering from what was, quite frankly, a rather intense rush. Sasha's long beanpole body wrapped up messily around mine was the finest thing I'd ever experienced up to that point in my life and I was in no hurry to move.

'I want to get a pizza,' she said out of nowhere.

'Um, okay, if you want.'

'I want a really disgusting oily, salty one with olives, anchovies, ham and extra cheese. We're going to eat it here in bed and then we're going to fuck again but we'll take it slower, okay?'

I had no argument against it. A pizza was duly ordered, Sasha went to the front door with a towel wrapped around her long body scandalizing both the delivery guy and the Taiwanese students who were by now gathered in the lounge room eating some sort of home made noodle thing.

In the morning I woke before Sasha in a state of quiet joy. Sasha was draped all over me. She had, and still has, a habit of sprawling her giraffe like body across me while we're asleep so that in the morning it looks like a spider has got halfway through devouring me and fallen asleep on the job. I enjoyed the sensation so much I didn't want to get up but my bladder forced the issue. I accidentally stepped on the empty pizza box when I untangled myself from her and got up. She stirred but didn't wake. I put on my pants and went out to have a piss.

The Taiwanese students were in the lounge room, drinking tea and having breakfast.

'Charlie and Charlie's friend!' One of them announced with a joyous smile in my direction. I knew then they'd heard it all last night. I gave them a thumbs up and went for my piss.

Life felt sweeter after this. I felt like something really good and meaningful had happened and there was some sort of destination that both Sasha and I were heading towards now. No more being lost dropkicks just getting by, we were together and had a shared destiny and it felt great.

Trevor knew as soon as I walked through into the KFC kitchen.

'You've fucked, haven't you?'

'Hello to you too, Trevor.'

'You're practically glowing, it's almost obscene. I assume it went well?'

'A gentleman never tells, Trevor.'

'Did you let your ferret out for a run? Judging by your radiant glow, I'd say so.'

'I have entered into a meaningful and loving relationship with a good woman who means a lot to me and said relationship does include a physical element, if that's what you mean, Trevor.'

'You've got your end away and your head is spinning, all well and good. But don't let it affect your recovery, okay?'

'Okay, Trevor.'

Life went on.

Sasha and I were even more joined at the hip now. We did everything together and it just felt right. Love gave life a glow it didn't have before.

About this time the suspension of my driver's license ended. I went through the rigmarole of getting it back, had to get a new photo and everything, but when it finally came, bright and shiny in the mail it was like I was reborn. There remained the problem of getting a car. I was going to go the cheapest option and get something secondhand but Sasha advised against it. I ended up getting a little hatchback, I didn't see the need for anything bigger, and used the dealer finance to do it. I was in debt like every other wage slave which was mildly worrying but on the other hand I was mobile again which was truly a joy.

The day I got the car I drove out to Semaphore beach with Sasha. It was too cold to swim still, we'd need at least another month of sunshine, but the simple act of walking on the beach holding her hand was as close to divine as I'd tasted in a long time.

After a few weeks of being a couple, I decided Sasha should meet my mum. We duly went up to Modbury one Sunday afternoon for lunch at Mum's place. My mum loved Sasha on sight and fussed over her like she was her own daughter.

Afterwards, I drove Sasha around the area showing her various things I remembered from growing up there. I don't think she'd ever been to Modbury before. I showed her the skate park and spotted old mate, still there, still hanging out after all these years. His hairline had receded even further, there were grey streaks sprinkled through and he didn't look healthy. But apparently none of this bothered him very much, he was still dressed in the same teenage fashion from twenty years ago, still living the same life.

I began to explain to Sasha as best I could.

'This guy used to hang here when I was a kid. It was actually him that made me think joining the Army was a good idea.'

'How? What did he say?'

'He didn't say anything really, it was just I could see him drifting his life away hanging around this skate park, drinking beer, smoking bongs, working some dead end job to pay for it all. I became worried that I was going to end up like him. So I decided that I needed to do something decisive. I joined the Army, and a fat lot of good that did me.'

I was silent for a few minutes thinking about all the time that had passed and all the things that had happened. I felt a little depressed. I still didn't really feel like I was winning at life after so much struggle and strife and here was old mate, who'd never put in the slightest effort in life, seemingly happy and content. Something wasn't right.

As if reading my thoughts Sasha touched my arm and brought me out of myself.

'Stop going over old choices and their consequences in your mind all the time. It does you no good. You were young, you made what seemed to be the right choice at the time. That's it. This guy made his choice. There isn't some final judge or arbitration on our lives, you don't get a ribbon or a dunce's hat at the end of your life based on the choices you made. It's just riding the waves as best you can. In the meantime, live and enjoy life.'

She squeezed my hand and smiled and I felt loved.

Then she started to speak in her best David Attenborough voice.

'Here we see the middle aged skate park flog in his natural habitat. Despite being older, this male still hangs around teenagers and occasionally attempts to mate with them.'

I laughed and decided to join in with my own David Attenborough voice.

'The middle-aged skate park flog attempts to impress the younger females with gifts of alcohol and displays his skating skills hoping she will decide to mate with him. Alas, this female is not interested.'

Sasha laughed with me and the day seemed bright again. We drove off leaving old mate to his skate park and his life.

The weather grew warmer. Summer was starting and Sasha and I were starting to think about the future a little.

Firstly, there was the issue of accommodation. Sasha was staying with me but her name wasn't on the lease so her position was precarious. Theoretically the landlord could chuck her out at any time. We decided to get a flat of our own.

'They want how much a week? Fuck me!' Rents had gone up since I had last rented a flat of my own.

'Well, between your KFC wage and my trust fund it's still doable. Don't worry, we'll manage.' Sasha said this with the confidence of someone who had never had to worry about money.

In the end we got a little place in Windsor Gardens not far from the Greenacres shopping centre. We said goodbye to the Taiwanese students and Churchill Road and moved in. It felt good, like life was progressing, like we were getting somewhere.

After a long day of setting up furniture and getting settled in we looked at our little slice of domesticity with a certain satisfaction.

'At last we can fuck without the Taiwanese students listening in. C'mon then.'

Sasha grabbed my hand and led me to bed. I didn't struggle against it.

Shortly after this Trevor invited us to his two years sober birthday at his Alcoholic Anonymous home group.

Sasha and I showed up and were by far the youngest people there. The guy leading the group started speaking about halfway through the meeting to announce Trevor's achievement.

'And by way of announcement, Trevor, you all know Trevor, don't you? Well, Trevor here is celebrating two years sober and –'

The group erupted in clapping and cheers of "good on ya, Trev!" which took a little bit to settle down. Evidently, Trevor was much loved in this group.

'And well, he's been a vital part of this group for two years and it's been a blessing to share his sobriety journey with him, so let's have a cheer for Trevor!'

Right on cue someone brought in a birthday cake with two candles on it. People started singing *Happy Birthday* and cheered loudly when Trevor blew out the candles. Trevor was asked to share.

'My name's Trevor and I'm an alcoholic.'

'Hi Trevor!' The group response was jolly and celebratory.

'Two years ago I had enough of drinking. I was beaten. I decided to give AA a go for three months and if it didn't work I was going to kill myself. Well, here I am, every day sober is a victory and a joy and I'm happy to be alive and sharing this journey with you fine people. God bless every one of you.'

He kept the same deadpan, carved in stone expression the whole time he was speaking.

'Does he ever smile?' Sasha whispered in my ear.

'Not that I've ever seen.'

We had some cake and stayed to chat after the meeting. It was a good day.

Summer kicked in and we started to swim a little. Sasha had the classic former junkie's paranoia about the various scars on her body from using. I reassured her that they were fading and could hardly be seen and anyway, nobody would notice.

She reluctantly bought a pair of bathers and we went to Largs Bay for a swim. It was glorious. She loosened up as she realised nobody was looking and nobody cared about some old and rapidly fading scars.

She dived under the water and swam towards me. She emerged from the sea like some pagan goddess of beauty and seafood, long, jet black hair streaming wet down her back. Her eyes locked onto mine and she put her arms around my shoulders and kissed me.

For a moment we stood there kissing gently in the water, sun streaming down on us.

'I love you, Charlie,' she said gently and sincerely.

'I love you, Sasha,' I said back equally sincerely.

We held each other for a long time and enjoyed the glorious sunshine and the salt water. I realised just how happy I was. More than that, I realised how I had never really planned any of my life and had just reacted to whatever seemed best at the time and had somehow ended up happy. Someone or something is looking over and blessing me for reasons I cannot begin to fathom. To whatever or whoever it is, I silently prayed, thank you for this life.

We swam most of the afternoon and we enjoyed every minute of it.

ACKNOWLEDGEMENTS

The author would like to thank his wife and daughter for their love and support, as well as the lads from Tooky's Mag, Book Club from Hell and Minimag for their enthusiasm and boosting.

The author would also like to thank Dirty Three whose album *Ocean Songs* he played a lot while writing this.

You'll Always Remember Fremantle was originally published in *&Amp Magazine*.

Also from Truth Serum Press by
Lewis Woolston

truthserumpress.net/catalogue/fiction/the-last-free-man-and-other-stories

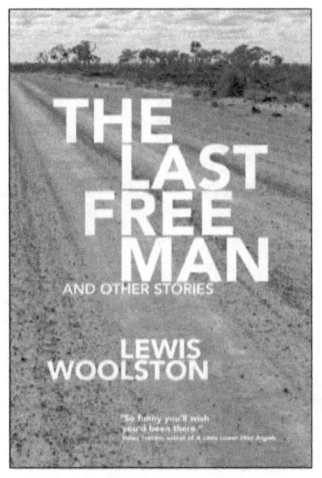

Shortlisted for 'Best Fiction' in the 2020 Chief Minister's NT Book Awards, *The Last Free Man and Other Stories* portrays characters who live in Australia's remotest areas. Many have chosen such a life, valuing independence and personal freedom above all else. Some have simply ended up there. Each story takes the reader inside the rhythms and mindset of his characters: Woolston's eye is curious and unobtrusive as he illuminates their quirks and impulses. The stories unfold with a confident sense of pace, and by the end of the collection, the reader has gained a vivid and often amusing insight into life in Australia's great outback. (*Imprint*, NT Writers' Centre)

Available in paperback and eBook.

www.ingramcontent.com/pod-product-compliance
Lightning Source LLC
Chambersburg PA
CBHW020651260626
47157CB00008B/2985